Enjo~ ~re!

Sierra Michaels

Breakfast in Bimini

by

Sierra Michaels

CONTENTS

ACKNOWLEDGMENTS

I would like to thank my editor Troy Lambert for his valuable advice in all areas of writing and publishing. Fellow writer Barbara Silkstone for her helpful insight on the publishing process. Jillian Morris for her beautiful photo of Bimini used as the book cover background. Elle J Rossi for cover design. Karen Chess, Eric Christy, Jillian Morris and Leesa Fountain for allowing me to bounce ideas off them. Most of all my husband, Brad, for his unconditional support in all my endeavors.

CHAPTER ONE

FORT LAUDERDALE TO BAHAMAS

MAY 26, 2011

Lucas woke me at sunrise, rolling over to deliver a light, gentle kiss to my lips. I turned toward him with a muted moan and a quick unconscious peck, swiftly retreating back into my subconscious dream-state. I always slept deeply next to him, feeling like I was protected by a mighty warrior. In his arms nothing could hurt me, not even my own nightmares, a feeling I previously hadn't experienced, and now welcomed. He quietly slid out of bed.

"Let's go. We can have breakfast in Bimini." He said, pleasantly reappearing a moment later in deep blue and yellow striped Hurley swim trunks and a sleeveless tan shirt exposing his muscular biceps. His sandy blonde hair was grown out and disheveled on the top, while precisely razor trimmed at the base of his skull.

"Wake up," he demanded, standing over the king-sized oak sleigh bed with arms akimbo.

Gently rubbing my eyes, I stretched my perpetually tight, aching thighs while slowly blinking into consciousness. Glancing up, I admired his smile filled with obvious anticipation, "Come on, sweetie. Get dressed."

"Okay." I muttered without moving, momentarily searching my mind for the remnants of a funky dream.

We were beginning a two-week private cruise through the Bahamas, joining some friends for a portion of the trip. We'd rented a two-bedroom houseboat in Miami along with another couple, who captained the vessel. They'd set sail days ago and would meet us in the capital of the island chain, Nassau. From there, we would cruise the outer islands with Lucas's newly acquired thirty-six-foot center console, an Intrepid, as the primary fishing craft and tender to the houseboat, a Bluewater.

The previous night we'd stocked his boat with water, beer, munchies, a cooler and our bags. Now half -asleep from our late night lovemaking session and contemplating our adventure, I jumped out of bed as thoughts of having breakfast in a foreign country cleared my groggy mind. We'd flown to Grand Bahama in his small plane a few times for a day or two, but this was our first sea voyage together to the islands.

"Good boat name, *Breakfast in Bimini.*" I mumbled, slipping into a periwinkle bikini top and jean shorts, automatically tying my thick auburn hair into a quick bun, securing it to the top of my head with a blue scrunchie, almost Buddha-like.

Lucas had only owned the boat for a week, so we'd been actively thinking about names, tossing around catchy phrases over drinks and trip preparations. Conveniently moored in a canal behind his house, over the past few days we checked and tested all electronics, radios, life vests, flares and lights.

"Can you grab the lunch meats, cheese and bags of ice, please?" He asked while preparing the helm.

After gathering the remaining supplies, I double checked locked doors, dimmed the lights and then slid out a side exit.

As we pulled away from the dock, romantic thoughts of the song "Breakfast at Tiffany's" played in my head. *"And I said, what about Breakfast in Bimini, and she said, I think I remember the film."* I changed the words to fit my version as I always did when songs taunted my mind. The song, a popular tune in the mid-1990s, was about a couple who had almost nothing in common, except they both liked the Audrey Hepburn film. Somehow love would find a way to make the relationship work.

Lucas and I had quite a lot in common, I concluded after a brief moment of reflection on the song. I'd felt comfortable hanging with him from the moment we'd met just six months ago, a few short weeks after I moved from San Pedro, California to Florida. I'd been working as an education director for the Graves Museum of Archaeology and Natural History in Fort Lauderdale, and Lucas had chaperoned his son's third grade class on a field trip. He kept asking me questions and seemed really interested in the tour. Afterward, he invited me to his house to join him and a handful of friends for a casual Sunday BBQ. We'd been inseparable ever since. I embraced his boating lifestyle as a newbie mariner, and he showed interest in my passion for archaeology, travel and flying. I was in the process of obtaining my pilot's license, and he jumped right in to obtain his as well. He was a natural navigator with over twenty years of boating experience, smoothly transitioning his expertise from the seas to the skies. We were teaching each other and finding love in the process, although I still had a lot to learn about seamanship and a fear of water to conquer.

Lucas called out from the boat, "Can you get the front line? I have the rear, and they're coming with us."

"Okay." After untangling the rope from the piling, I jumped onboard secretly hoping my commitment to a few weeks at sea was wise. Unlike Lucas, I wasn't at one with the ocean. I found it fascinating, but dangerous. I didn't desire to explore its depth without gills, yet I felt brave and ready for a new adventure, a voyage into the unknown.

While cruising the Intercostal waterway toward the Hillsboro Inlet, I organized the vessel for the two-hour crossing from Fort Lauderdale to Bimini. Having breakfast in the Bahamas intrigued me. After all, how often can you wake up in the states, spend a few hours traversing international waters and arrive in another country at an hour when most people were just getting to work?

"So what kind of breakfast do they have in the Bahamas?" I asked nonchalantly as we departed the inlet, speeding full throttle into the ocean.

"They have great pancakes and omelets," he said without turning his head. "It's not very different from the U.S., just a good break where we can check in and relax before pressing on." He stood erect at the helm focusing on his heading and the seas, while I sat next to him. "Andros is our destination for the night."

"Are you going to dive the wall?" I asked, referring to the large barrier reef located just off Andros.

"Not unless you join me."

My sideways glance went unnoticed with Lucas intensely focused on the water. "Honey, you know I can't swim well. And I've never been diving."

"Good thing I was a lifeguard in college. You have your own private rescuer in case there's a problem." His eyes shifted briefly toward mine. "And you know I'm not going to let anything happen to you."

I smiled unexpectedly at his protective side, instinctively knowing his affectionate nature from the moment we met.

We headed in a southeast direction as I peered out to sea, looking for hints of the marine life thriving below. The ocean appeared calm and glassy. Emerging sunlight caused a glistening of the sea's surface as if it rained silver glitter the previous night. Flying fish teased the boat. Fort Lauderdale and Miami disappeared on the horizon while Jimmy Buffett blared from the speakers. We sipped cappuccino-colored coffee while admiring pelicans and frigate birds high above the Gulf Stream. The salty smell of the sea permeated the air. Breakfast would be just the beginning of our two-week expedition.

A large freighter in the distance passed from south to north, creating a gentle swell in the otherwise serene water. I imagined Ponce de Leon traveling the same Gulf Stream current hundreds of years ago.

Two hours seemed to take no time at all and we arrived at Bimini Sands, a resort and restaurant just fifty miles west of Miami. It was still early in my current world, and the inhabitants were just starting to stir on the island. However, I was awake, hungry, and ready to explore.

We drifted into the marina, each lighting a cigarette prior to docking. Lucas pointed to the second floor of a bright-coral octagon building. "The restaurant's up there, the Petite Conch."

"Cute name."

He motioned towards a smaller one-story structure. "We have to clear customs first."

After glancing at the sign, I jumped on the dock grabbing the ropes he threw to me. We secured them to the cleats and headed toward the office. Two uniformed agents, one for customs and one for immigration, checked our paperwork. I handled getting our passports stamped while Lucas paid the fee for a cruising permit.

At the restaurant I ordered pancakes and Lucas opted for an omelet with cheese, a side of bacon and hash browns. Over six feet tall with a muscular frame he could afford a large meal from time to time. On the other hand, I had a smaller physique and the pancakes would just sit in my belly for the rest of the day. I would probably only make it through one if they were IHOP sized, especially since I hadn't run this morning.

"Service in the Bahamas is slow," he said, flashing a loving grin.

"Can we walk along the beach while we wait?" I begged, tilting my head.

"Sure." He called the waitress over and let her know our plans to return in a half-hour.

"No problem, mon." She said in a thick Bahamian dialect.

We strolled hand in hand around the marina admiring the crystal clear turquoise water. Jellyfish pulsated in unison, clustered in small groups. They were transparent pink with a design similar to a four-leaf clover in the center, except more rounded. Some floated upside down exposing their tentacles while taking in salt water to the rhythm of a heartbeat, graceful like ballerinas in Tchaikovsky's *Swan Lake*. A long barracuda swam through the jellies, clumsy and vicious looking. Its perpetual smile exposed big teeth, eyeballing me like its next meal.

"A barracuda is staring at me," I said, staring back.

"It's harmless. The locals here eat them."

"Yuck." I scrunched my face. "What do they taste like?"

"I wouldn't know. I'm picky about my fish." Gently pulling me away from the marina, "They have a beautiful beach over here."

At a small beach I started looking for shells. I rummaged through pieces in the sand, hoping to find a nice souvenir from our morning stop in Bimini. The wind blew lightly from the southwest. As I was searching, I spotted what appeared to be a carved wooden ball. I began eagerly digging around it with my fingers, exposing a head attached to a back with side arms, buttocks and legs. An intact statue lay horizontally on the sand, face down.

I set it upright. It stood about two feet high and appeared very primitive. A hairline framed his face with straight lines etched as hair wrapping around elongated ears, one fully carved eye orb the other half shaped as if winking, a wide flat nose, and a small mouth with a full lower lip. An opening the size of a nickel had been carved in the top center of his head.

5

The body revealed a muscular chest, a thinner waist with bent elbows by its side, robust thighs and butt and a single wide foot. His average sized genitals were exposed. Its right leg bent at the knee and a circular hole replaced a missing foot.

Was it attached to something? I wondered. The left arm also had a perfectly round etching in place of a hand. *What did it once hold?* It seemed in good condition, with only a few small barnacles clinging to crevices in the wood.

I picked up the piece and ran over to Lucas who was standing near some bulky rocks jutting into the sea.

"Look what I found," I shouted, waving the statue in the air.

His eyes widened. "Wow. Nice."

Handing it over, I asked, "Where do you think it came from?" I tilted my head waiting for his reply.

"Well the current flows north, so perhaps Cuba." He handed it back.

I studied the statue. "It doesn't appear Cuban. Look at the eyes and nose. The features are more African." I tilted the figurine forward toward Lucas. "And there's a large hole at the top of his head, as if it was attached to something." I rotated it, showing its backside. "And the leg, a smaller one, the size of a jelly belly."

He glanced at it again and smirked. "Raves, you're the archaeologist. Research it. You always welcome a challenge." He looked out to sea, pushing his chin in the same direction. "Have you heard of the Bimini Road?"

"I've heard of it. Some think it's the lost city of Atlantis." I also stared into the distance. "I've seen pictures, a J-shaped road with large boulders. It looks like a natural formation in the photos."

He pointed northwest. "It's in the shallow waters just over there. Off North Bimini, near those three large rocks."

"Have you seen it?

"I dove it once looking for lobster. The stones make great ledges where they hide. I speared enough for a nice dinner."

I chuckled, leaning over and lightly kissing him on the lips with a soft, "Do you think breakfast is ready yet?"

"Let's find out." He grabbed my hand and I proudly carried the statue back to the restaurant.

My stack of pancakes seemed like Mount Everest. I poured on the syrup and dug in, only making it through half. I pushed my plate toward Lucas, "Would you like a bite?"

He finished his plate, then took a small sample. "That's really good." He tilted his head, leaning in and gazing with his gentle green eyes. "Honey, you didn't eat much. Is it enough for you? It's a long ride." He pushed the plate back towards me.

I patted my belly. "I'm stuffed. Really. And besides, we have snacks on the boat for later."

"Let's get going then. We'll be back here for a longer stay at the end of the trip."

Jumping into the boat I started the engines while Lucas untied it. After placing the statue in the cuddy cabin next to our bags, I fiddled with my iPod. "What do you want to listen to? Buffett again?"

"Okay for now. We may want to change it up a bit half-way through. I don't know if I can listen to the same music for four hours."

I cranked the music and found a comfortable spot on a sunny cushion, taking the opportunity to work on my tan. Bouncing by the small island of South Bimini, I admired the colorful houses lining the rocky shoreline: a lime-green house followed by a two-story sky-blue one, a cute peach house with a separate tiki hut, and an out-of-place rock house. They all must have had killer views. The island ended at a point where a modest restaurant sat perched above the beach rock.

A mammoth dilapidated ship rested offshore. Aiming my index finger in its direction while shouting, "What's that?"

"The concrete ship."

Joining Lucas to get a better view of the monstrosity, I said, "It looks pretty old and battered."

"It is, from the 20's I think. He slowed to trolling speed so I could take a picture. He lifted his chest, rooster-like with his hands on his hips. "That ship was a rum runner back in the day, and pilots used it for target practice during WW II. I'm sure it endured many hurricanes. Nowadays, it's a popular spot for snorkeling and diving."

Graffiti covered the bow, and the stern was missing. It had an open center exposing steel supports inside, equally spaced and resembling baby back ribs.

We sped up, passing a few more small islands with boats circling around them, and then reached the open ocean. After some hours passed, the boat slowed and I joined Lucas near the controls.

Without the wind I felt my skin burning in the intense sun. "Hey, baby, why are we stopping?"

"I want to take a quick break and grab a beer." Gliding to the back of the boat, he lifted two bottles from the cooler, and handed me one.

Clicking my beer to his, I said, "To our adventure. There's really nothing out here, is there? I mean between Bimini and Andros?"

He lit two cigarettes, passing one to me and taking a long draw. "Just ocean creatures, submarines and pirates."

I burst out laughing, puffing out a cloud of smoke. "What, Blackbeard, lost WWII German fighters and the Lock Ness monster? Perhaps my statue came from Blackbeard's ship."

He smiled at my amusement, but I could see his humorless eyes through his sunglasses. "I'm serious. The US Navy does submarine testing out here and Andros is famous for harboring pirates-they steal boats from all over the Bahamas."

"Sorry honey, I didn't mean to offend you. It just sounded funny."

He lightly slapped my butt, wickedly grinning. "I know you're a smart ass. It's one of the things I love about you."

I snickered, feeling my cheeks flush with the mention of I, love, and you in the same sentence.

"What about sea creatures?" I teased. His passion for the ocean ran deep, especially in Bahamian waters, and I enjoyed provoking his enthusiasm.

He put his cigarette butt into an empty beer bottle. "I'm not referring to mythical monsters, but real ocean life. These waters are loaded with fish, whales, porpoises, and sharks. We probably don't have to worry about subs or pirates until tomorrow. They're generally south of where we're going tonight. Ready to press on?"

Lucas confidently stood, navigating while I sat next to him. I felt more aware of the possibilities under the sea and searched for any signs of life. The ocean floor was probably littered with artifacts from the 16th and 17th centuries when ships traversed the region, trading goods from the New World to the Old and vice versa.

"How deep is it here?" I asked loudly.

"About twenty feet," he answered after a brief glance at his depth finder. "It's going to drop to about 6,000 shortly and then become shallow again as we approach Andros." He pointed straight ahead. "There's the northeast tip."

I stood up for a better view and squinted. "I think I see it." Would you like another beer?"

"Yes. Please."

Carefully teetering to the cooler on the stern, I first squatted to tinkle, crouching off the back platform while hovering over the water and holding a rail. When nature called fearlessness took over. When I finished, I pulled out two Kalik lights and made my way back to Lucas, as if doing a balancing act on a tight rope, clearly not used to bouncing and walking at the same time.

"Six-thousand feet." He called out. "We're in the Tongue of the Ocean briefly to get around some reefs. Tomorrow we'll be in the deep water until we get to Nassau."

"Sweet." I hung my head over the side, peering into the sapphire sea, mesmerized by its depth and color as translucent and solid as the gemstone on my middle finger. The water seemed unyielding at first glance, but upon further examination I noticed the water's diaphanous character. Then, without warning a dolphin shot into the air with a graceful flip and dove back into the ocean.

"Wow." I clapped my hands as Lucas slowed down to a snail's pace. Two more leapt from the water, and started playing with the bow of our Intrepid. I crawled up front, cheering them on as they effortlessly shot back and forth in front of the boat. "We're not going to run them over, right?"

He smirked. "No. They're very smart, just playful."

I watched and sought a connection. I wanted to swim with them, but jumping into the deep sea terrified me. They played in our wake, then I got a joyful glance just prior to another 180 flip into the air. She smiled. At least I thought of this one as a she, I couldn't tell the difference between the sexes, but the gracefulness of these creatures appeared more feminine than masculine. I smiled back and naturally started cheering.

"Beautiful. Do it again." Another aerial somersaulted above the waves.

I adored dolphins. I recalled hearing they formed strong long-lasting bonds. I secretly hoped Lucas and I were developing a similar lifelong relationship. They disappeared into their lighthearted world.

"Wow, what a spectacular show, I said." Lucas increased speed with a smile and moved on.

A few miles out from Morgan's Bluff Lucas radioed Kate's Landing for navigation instructions into the harbor, where we would anchor for the night. As we traversed towards land he explained the set-up from his past trips.

Kate's was a small bed and breakfast located on a remote part of Andros, owned and operated by a fascinating Norwegian woman who'd relocated to the island decades ago, along with the help of her Bahamian boyfriend, Duff. Together, they owned their personal house, two villas and a larger rental with six bunk beds, a kitchen, and a family room. We'd rented one of the cottages. So we anchored just a few feet from the shoreline behind the reef protecting the beach, then waded through the water to arrive at our home for the night.

Kate and Duff greeted us at the water's edge. "Can we help you carry anything?" Kate asked.

"No thanks, we travel light." Lucas said. I had my backpack hanging on my shoulder and he carried a small duffle bag and cooler. Lucas shook Duff's hand, then gave Kate a light embrace. He glanced at me with a fervent nod and smiled. "This is my girlfriend, Raves."

Kate hugged me and grinned, "Welcome to our humble abode." She was petite with blondish grey hair, short and naturally styled framing her warm face. She reminded me of a younger, thinner Betty White. In contrast, Duff stood as tall as Lucas. He had a sharp jaw line, a tiny patch of grey near the front of his curly hair, a beautiful chocolate brown complexion, and appeared very toned for his age. The pair radiated affection and hospitality.

"Thanks for helping us into the harbor," Lucas said as we all headed for the main house. "This is a complicated cove to navigate without proper maps."

"And it's always changing with each storm we get, so a map isn't very useful." Kate responded.

Two large dogs greeted us, a bigger black one and a friendly tan canine named Dancer. They were potcakes, the local Bahamian hybrid similar to a shepherd lab mix. The breed got their quirky name from feeding on the rice and pea leftovers from a traditional Bahamian meal. Dancer pranced around our feet, leading us to our cottage.

"Here are your accommodations for the night." Kate said as she opened the door, extending her arm for us to enter. Duff and the black dog had disappeared during our journey, detouring to a neighboring bungalow. "When you get settled, come join us for a drink at the main house." Kate and Dancer left together and then we semi-unpacked.

I pulled out my running clothes for the morning, placing them on the dresser along with my iPod and sunscreen. I changed into my jeans and a turquoise halter, then sat on the bed inspecting the beauty surrounding me while waiting for Lucas. The room was bright and cozy, tropically decorated, yet it could have easily fit into the landscape of coastal Maine. Sailing and fishing art decorated the walls, and a bookshelf held a variety of titles including romance, action, business, fishing, and books on sailing the world.

Lucas emerged freshly showered sporting long khaki shorts and a white linen button down shirt unbuttoned to reveal the upper portion of his curly chest hairs.

"Nice threads," I commented, glancing up from the bed. "Are we going somewhere special for dinner?"

"Yes, Kate's Landing." He said sincerely. "This part of Andros is residential."

"Let's take a walk around," I urged.

His green eyes sparkled. "Sounds good." He placed my hand in his, "I like to stretch my legs after a full day on the water."

We walked down a heavily pitted dirt road littered with potholes. It appeared to have been partially paved at some point in its history, or maybe the natural bedrock had just worn down through the decades. Large houses sporting well-groomed yards devoid of any signs of life sat idle. They did not seem abandoned, just quiet with no trash, cars, pets or open doors visible.

"These homes look empty." I said. "I guess they're vacation homes?"

"I think most are owned by Americans. I'd like to have a vacation house here at some point. I'm not sure what island, yet. But Andros is a possibility." He squeezed my hand a bit tighter. "Maybe we can decide together some day."

My heart warmed. "I'd love to share a home with you."

He did a graceful U-turn as I organically rotated with him. "On most of these islands the locals live closer to town. It's easier to get around and it's a bit more convenient with restaurants and grocery stores nearby. We'll have plenty of chances to eat local cuisine. Around here it tends to be all fried."

I had an aversion to fried food. I'd try it, but in limited amounts. I preferred fresh naturally lean foods.

We stopped back at the cottage to pick up a bottle of vodka and some wine from the cooler for dinner. I checked out the bathroom, finding it equally as colorful as the rest of the cottage, but tiny by American standards. The small space housed a shower and toilet catty-corner behind a hidden sliding wooden door. A typed laminated sign above the toilet read, "If its yellow let it mellow, if its brown flush it down." In the entryway between the bathroom and bedroom, in front of the main door, sat the sink, a mirror and a coffee-maker.

I put my arm through Lucas' as we sauntered barefoot over the Bermuda grass to the back porch of Kate's house. We joined the two, already sitting outside. "Where can I find a wine opener and a few glasses?" Lucas asked.

"This way," Duff said, taking Lucas inside.

"I love the landscaping here and the grass. It's so soft on the feet. Is it hard to grow?" I asked Kate, as I lit a cigarette.

"It seems to grow with little effort. It holds true for the trees and shrubs I have on the property. They're all native."

I scanned the huge yard which faded into the ebb and flow of the ocean. Bermuda grass mottled with sand covered the lawn, which was dotted with scattered palm trees, a few bushes and driftwood. Hammocks were tied between trees and brightly painted wooden chairs decorated the landscape. Wispy cirrus clouds brushed the horizon, and I anticipated a beautiful sunset. Only the purr of small waves filled the air. No sounds of cars, planes, boats or sirens invaded our space.

"I saw all your sailing boats in the cottage, did you discover Andros while sailing?" I asked.

"I do love sailing, and I've been around the world. I settled here because my ex-husband worked at the Navy's AUTEC facility. We moved here about twenty-five years ago. The kids got older, we grew apart and went our separate ways. I opened the bed and breakfast after our split."

"It's a lovely and peaceful place. Is business good?"

"Oh yes, all of our weekends are booked over the next few months. You two were lucky to arrive on a weekday. Even then sometimes we're sold out. Business has been wonderful and the internet has helped boost our rentals, as we received good reviews and the visitors post great photos."

"Is it mostly fishermen? It seems too remote for others to find."

"Morgan's Bluff is a bonefishing destination. Duff manages the excursions for most of our guests. It's mostly American fishermen and families, but quite a few Europeans visit. We have a small airport, and they can take a taxi here or I pick them up."

Lucas returned, handing me a glass of Pinot Grigio.

"Raves is an interesting name. I don't think I've heard it before. Does it have a certain origin?" Kate asked.

"It's short for Raven. I'm part Native American. For certain tribes the Raven is considered a bringer of light." I crushed my cigarette in Kate's ashtray.

"I thought ravens and crows corresponded to bad luck?"

"Among the Pueblo tribes it's considered a venerated bird of creation." I smiled at Kate, pausing for a moment. "If my name means bad luck then I'm screwed."

Lucas laughed. "Speaking of luck, did you tell Kate about the statue you found?"

"Maybe it's better if I show her. I'll be back." I set down my glass on a translucent table. Briskly walking to the shoreline, I rolled up my jeans and waded to the boat. When I picked up the statue from the cabin I felt a strong, unusual energy. It felt like an electrical current passed through my body, momentarily leaving me paralyzed. At the same time, I noticed a faint green glow around the boat. "Strange," I said aloud.

Returning to the threesome, I held up my prize. "What do you think?"

Kate's eyes widened while Duff's remained unchanged. "What a curious piece," Kate responded as I handed it over.

"I found it on the beach in Bimini. It's in good shape, with just a few small barnacles. It's not waterlogged, so it probably spent a limited time in the ocean. Weeks, or at most a month or two, no longer." I said, searching for her reaction. "Any thoughts on where it might have come from?"

She examined its features. "Well, I've never seen anything like it. The barnacles are small but there are quite a few, so from my experience it means the idol was probably in the water a few weeks."

"I think it's some sort of religious idol too." I responded enthusiastically. To hear it from someone else made my heart race.

"Well, it's my first hunch. But it could be anything. With the time it probably spent in the water, it could have come from Cuba."

Lucas grinned and chuckled. "That's what I said. The Gulf Stream current runs from south to north."

I took a leisurely sip of wine. "You could both be right. But the features don't look Cuban to me. Of course I haven't been there, but I have spent some time in Africa and the art style is similar. With its exposed genitals, I'd say it could be a fertility symbol of some sort. Except I'd think they'd be bigger."

Duff quietly disappeared inside while Kate handed the statue back to me, smiling, "Sounds like you two should visit Cuba on a quest, since it's close."

I placed the statue on the ground, next to my chair and contemplated a trip to Cuba. It would be my type of adventure, filled with exploration and potential danger. Seeking out answers on a potentially ancient artifact, yet forbidden by our government to visit Castro's island. I tuned into the conversation Lucas and Kate were engaged in about Bahamian politics. I interrupted at what I considered to be an appropriate break.

"So Kate, have you been to Cuba?"

"Oh, yes. A few times." She answered with a big grin. "It's easy to get there from Nassau, and our government has decent relations with them." She carefully lit a cigarette and took a baby sip of wine. I did the same, and she described her experience. "My first time I arrived in Havana with my ex-husband by sailboat. They have a huge port compared to the ones in the Bahamas. We found a slip for a few nights and explored old Havana. It was like a step back in time. The cars are from the 50's for the most part and the architecture is elegant and full of history."

"Do you speak Spanish?" I inquired.

She looked at Lucas then me. "Enough to get by. Many people there speak English."

I glanced at Lucas, showing him the adventurous longing in my eyes. "No." He blurted out. "Not this trip and not by boat."

Kate laughed. "You can take a flight from Nassau, it's easy from there. It's an interesting place, and you might find some answers to the origin of your idol." I needed no convincing, but

I'm glad Lucas heard the urging from someone we both respected.

"I agree," I responded, then clarified. "Not tomorrow or anything, but sometime soon."

"I'll consider it. But I don't like the idea of being in a country we're not supposed to visit. If something goes wrong, we're on our own."

"Okay, kids. I'm going to prepare dinner," Kate said, standing up.

"Do you need help?" I inquired.

"Not at the moment," she said, gliding into the galley.

We wandered around the property, then Lucas settled into a hammock for a prime view of the sunset. I leaped on top of him and the hammock flipped, spilling us both onto the Bermuda grass where we stayed. I giggled. He shot me a smile. I kept giggling, then put my head on his chest. "This is a great view of the sunset right here." We glanced over the water at the burning disc slipping into the sea. I listened to him breathe in rhythm with the tender wind as I closed my eyes briefly.

When I retrieved the statue from the boat, I'd felt an energy I've never experienced before. Perhaps a sixth sense? I needed to find out where the statue came from and what its function had been. My intuition led me to believe it wasn't used for ordinary religious activities.

CHAPTER TWO

MAY 27, 2011

ANDROS TO NASSAU

The sun peeked through the blinds as a distant rooster crowed reminding me I wasn't in Florida. For a sleepy second I couldn't recall where I was. I opened the shades slightly, brewed some coffee then returned to bed. A delicate wind swayed the palm trees outside our window, and in the distance the once calm ocean showed a light chop. Lucas shifted like a yogi awakening from meditation. He slowly moved his fingers, toes and finally his long eyelashes blinked a few times. I put my face an inch from his, "Good morning sunshine." He gave me a blank stare and a polite smile. "You are totally more laid-back than yesterday morning when you told me to get up. I like this tranquil island side of you better."

"I feel completely relaxed after a good night's sleep."

"Would you like your cup of coffee in bed or outside on the lawn?" I asked getting up to pour.

Propping his elbows on the bed and scanning the bedroom he murmured, "I'd really like a TV to watch the news."

"Come on. Forget about it for a few days." I headed for the door with both cups in my hand. "There's nothing important you need to know first thing in the morning. Let's sit outside and admire the beauty, instead of hearing about all the chaos in the world." I opened the door, pushing on the handle with my elbow while kicking the bottom with my foot, glancing back to make sure he followed. Pulling on his boxers he trailed behind like a lethargic puppy.

"There could be a hurricane brewing," he said, sitting down on the picnic bench. "The wind has picked up since yesterday. Perhaps your idol is bringing bad juju our way."

I snickered, unconsciously blowing on my hot coffee "I don't believe in the supernatural, or numen."

"What's a numen?"

"A spirit inhabiting an object. But I have to admit, a strange feeling came over me when I picked up the statue yesterday. I need to research where it could have come from."

"See."

"So what are our plans for today?" I asked, to get an idea of departure time.

"Well, no real hurry," he said while swirling his coffee in the Styrofoam cup and taking a fleeting sip. "You can go for your run and I'll walk. I'll check email, weather, and so forth. Then we'll head towards Nassau. Jamie and Nick should already be there waiting for us with the larger boat."

"It's a Bluewater, right?"

"Yes, seventy-five footer. We'll use it as our base for cruising the Outer Islands and tow the intrepid for excursions."

I felt my heart race in excitement and took a large gulp of my now lukewarm caffeine, "Sweet. I'm going to get ready for my run."

I stopped by the main house to ask Kate about a good running route. Apparently, the only choice I had was to take a left turn and run straight out. She suggested I take Dancer since he "loved to run."

I didn't have to coach the potcake. He just knew what to do, and followed me to the main road, then led the way. I navigated potholes the size of moon craters, giving me a bit more side to side action like a crab. The petite pooch danced around them, sometimes even in and then back out of them. He'd disappear then reappear, looking back to make sure I didn't get lost. Sagebrush overgrowth lined the street, then a well-groomed house would materialize followed by more overgrowth. This continued for about two miles until we hit a busy intersection. Dancer recognized it and turned around, so I followed his direction as he safely returned me to his villa.

Lucas had been very productive while I ran. He confirmed good weather with a light chop along our route. Also, Jamie and Nick Kramer were waiting on the yacht at Paradise Island, the boat already fully stocked for our journey. They would probably be hanging at the pool or casino, depending upon our arrival time.

I used Kate's computer to search for any leads on the idol. After fifteen minutes browsing images of idols, dolls, and statues from the Bahamas and Cuba, I found nothing looking even remotely like my statue. Her sluggish internet prevented me from wanting to do additional research. I knew a search on African idols would produce numerous results, and I'd need more time and a faster connection to explore them.

Our gracious hosts walked with us to the water's edge, we exchanged hugs and kisses then waded through the shallow sea, climbing aboard the Intrepid with our bags.

"Let me know if you visit Cuba. I can give you some pointers and places to go." Kate called.

"We will," I shouted back.

We headed southeast, towards New Providence Island and the Bahamian capital of Nassau. Already burned out on Jimmy Buffett, I plugged in a general country mix into my iPod connected to the radio, and a comfortably snuggled into a bean bag chair. The island faded in the distance, not quite disappearing as the trees became matchsticks and the shoreline blurred.

I perused an old National Geographic magazine. I never threw them out, and had a complete collection dating back to 1961 with one issue as old as 1936. I inherited them from my mother's dad. This one was more recent, 2007. My mind wandered away from the magazine to the idol. A significant ancient artifact. I imagined. If the statue could talk and tell me his story, I was sure it would surpass my limited time at sea.

Soon after I began reading, Lucas screeched "Woo-hoo" and slowed the boat. He started snatching fishing rods calling out, "Take the helm. Keep us on a heading of 110."

Tossing my magazine, I rushed to the controls, "What do we have? Wahoo?" I shouted while trying to determine which way to move the wheel to stay on a 110 heading. A little to the right, a little to the left and so on. It felt as if I were steering a bobsled on an oil slick.

"Dolphinfish. Keep our heading," Lucas yelled as fishing lines whizzed out behind me. Standing on the foot bar I carefully studied the compass. "Pick up the pace," he shouted. "Just a hair on the right throttle then the left." I did as he requested. The whizzing sound increased to a roar as I quickly looked back to see Lucas grab the rod and start reeling.

"You got one?" I asked in a high voice.

"Of course honey. Just keep us straight, so the lines don't tangle."

I concentrated on the compass and heading and before I knew it Lucas threw a hefty big-headed tri-color fish from his gaff into the cooler. It was bright yellowish blue-green and blood dripped all over him and the boat. It could have easily been a scene from *The Texas Chainsaw Massacre*.

I heard some garble on the VHF, so I turned it down as my gaze drifted from the compass to Lucas. "Is that necessary?" I heard myself ask.

"What?" he said, perplexed.

I glimpsed ahead, then back as the fish started banging against the box in a final protest. Lucas sat on the cooler attempting to muffle its rage. "All the blood. It looks like a murder scene. Can you put it out of its misery?"

The fish eventually silenced, and Lucas shot me a sheepish look. "You like mahi-mahi, right?"

I sneered and got the Intrepid back on heading as Lucas quickly rinsed the blood from the boat and reset the lines. The ocean current and our slow toll helped drag the lures to a distance he deemed appropriate to keep the fish away from the engine noise, yet close enough to see the lure bobbing on the surface.

Joining me he took the helm. "You didn't answer my question."

"I've only had mahi-mahi a few times. And yes they're good, but I've never seen them caught. So I reserve the right to change my mind. I think gaffing his head is cheating. Can't you just reel until you win the fight? It's supposed to be a sport, right?"

Looking at me incredulity, he doubled over with laughter. "That's a good one. A bloody fish gets you all roused. But dragging around an idol with funky juju doesn't bother you." Bouts of giggles continued as we steadily trolled the water.

"I'm serious…" I felt a rumble as a rogue wave appeared from nowhere. Glancing over the stern I witnessed a black vessel the size of a small island break the surface. "Holy shit," I said.

He intuitively increased speed, not full throttle but enough to make it feel like we were fugitives escaping Alcatraz. "This hasn't happened to me before," he responded. "I've been called by submarines in this area, but never chased by one."

"Okay. It's a sub, good to know. They're on our side I'm presuming, so no torpedoes should be expected?" After looking behind and noticing the lures wildly bouncing out of the sea, I gently touched his side. "I don't think they're chasing us."

He checked behind us again and slowed down slightly. "I know." Glimpsing behind again, "It just took me by surprise."

Suddenly remembering I turned down the VHF I quickly reached to restore it. "The radio is back up."

"What?"

"I turned down the radio when I was concentrating on keeping the boat on heading and with all the chaos…"

Another look of disbelief crossed his face. "Well it explains why they didn't call." Reaching for the VHF, "AUTEC. I'm in a thirty-six-foot Intrepid about ten miles southeast of Morgan's Bluff. Have you been trying to contact me?"

I waved to the sub with a big smile. Lucas nudged me with a quick, "Stop it."

A serious deep voice bellowed through the VHF. "Yes captain. I've been trying to call you. We are conducting maneuvers in the area and we need you to leave immediately. Your heading is fine. Just pick up the pace."

"I'm reeling in my lines now, then we're on our way."

Lucas hurried to the stern, and said, "Don't touch the radio and just keep the boat straight."

"Yes sir, I shot back. "Can I take a picture of the sub first?" No response left me with the impression I shouldn't. It seemed colossal next to our vessel and it was the only other object in sight. It looked massive, long and surprisingly flat, with over half of its exterior still submerged. A tower rose with a recognizable periscope and painted white numbers I couldn't quite make out, 5 something maybe. The bright lettering was the only part of the vessel not pitch black. In stark contrast, its wake created a frosty foam. The entire scene turned me on, to my astonishment awakening my lust. I didn't know submarines sexually excited me until now. Concentrating on our heading, I stared ahead as buzzing reels echoed from behind.

"Throttle forward slightly." Lucas commanded.

Advancing the left engine then the right, I hollered back, "Is that good?"

Jumping beside me, dripping in sweat Lucas took the helm and within seconds we were soaring full speed ahead.

"Can I get you a towel?" I asked to ease the tension. Again, he didn't answer. I didn't think the question was inappropriate, but I sat silently as the boat bounced through the sea.

How cool, we saw a real submarine, I thought. The commander of the sub had an accent, it sounded German. A leftover from the war, I imagined. I giggled at the thought. I guess the Navy collaborates with our allies for training.

Finally slowing down a bit and breaking the silence, he said, "Honey, I love you but please don't turn down the VHF or wave at a sub again," he said calmly. "It's kind of eerie that the moment I mentioned bad juju the sub surfaced."

Dismissing the paranormal reference, I muttered, "Sorry," while looking up at him with a slight pout. "I found it exciting more than serious. Like we should ask them if they mind a photo or two before going on our way. They knew we were there. It's not like they popped up from underneath us."

"It's exactly what they did." Turning towards me mouth ajar, "Imagine if you were flying and I turned down the radio."

I'm pretty sure he has, I thought but instead responded, "I see your point, but legally, I need two-way communication in certain airspace. Are they required when boating?"

Shooting me a sideways look he said, "It's a safety concern."

"Okay, it won't happen again. Perhaps you can teach me more about the gauges and controls while we're out here, and I can be your co-captain. But I need to know more than just heading and how to handle the throttle." I scooted closer and said, "I already have an advantage being a pilot, right?"

Finally he offered a faint smile, "Yes, I can show you a few things."

Lucas has owned a boat since college, over fifteen years now. He knew every type of boat and engine, their average cost, the mechanics involved with each, and how to troubleshoot problems while at sea. He obtained his pilot's license about a month after I completed my training. With his background, going from ocean to air was an easy jump, taking half as long as I did transitioning the other way. Albeit I helped him with the written part, lending him my notes and quizzing him with easy ways to memorize certain answers. We both knew where to look for the information in the numerous books we carried inflight. Urgencies such as a fire or engine failure were memorized with a backup checklist in the cockpit.

I had limited boating experience prior to moving to Florida, only brief ferry rides in exotic locations, and a riverboat cruise on the Nile, all in calm water and land within sight, I focused more on the view than the instruments. When I started flying, I had to learn the effects of wind and weather on the airplane and terms such as rudder, trim and throttle. Applying this knowledge to boating worked to my advantage.

Standing at the controls, I monitored our heading of 120 and a steady speed of thirty knots. Being comfortable and familiar with those two gauges I began to scan the others. I figured out the GPS immediately: just follow the blue line. Fuel gauges were a no brainer with one for each engine, indicating the level of each tank. My gaze shifted to a basic black box with sharp green zig zag lines on the screen, followed by a flat line similar to a heart rate monitor I recalled seeing as a child during my brief visit to the ER. The bold numbers indicated 2653. I pointed and asked, "What's this?"

"Depth finder."

I glimpsed at the screen again. The jagged and horizontal lines turned into gentle waves. "So when the line shoots up and down does it indicate a dramatic change in depth?"

"Exactly." Can you slow down to about eight knots?" Wandering to the back of the boat he returned with two beers. "It's useful for fishing and navigation. It uses radio signals to detect objects not on the ground."

I noticed animated fish going across the screen. "So would it detect a submarine?" I asked, tilting my head slightly.

He snickered. "Simple depth finders don't have the range." He bumped my hip seizing back the helm. "I'll take over. We're less than forty minutes from port."

I climbed onto the bean bag to catch some rays, drinking a beer and singing *it's five O'clock somewhere.*

Could the idol seriously have magical power? Maybe part of a religious ritual? I recalled an experience in Benin, Africa where I had the opportunity to work on an international excavation. During my visit I attended a voodoo ceremony, one of only a few westerners. A masked man ran around an arena, dancing in a trance-like state. It was believed if he physically made contact, then whomever he touched would be doomed. Everyone ran, except me, confident in my disbelief I stayed put. My African brothers, as I referred to the four local archaeology students, formed a barricade protecting me and moving me to a secure room housing the elderly and children, where we could observe without risk. For the locals, it was a terrifying yet important part of their religion and culture. The masked man sensed my confidence, singling and taunting me. He touched me with his index finger for a brief moment, undetected by those with me. Did this momentary contact jinx me? *Nonsense.*

"Raves, are you wearing sunscreen? You're getting a little red."

"I'm supposed to, I'm part Native American. Remember." I hollered back, peeking under my bikini bottom.

My color, I attributed to my Hopi genes, a blessing from my father. At least it's what I understood from my limited knowledge of him. "His damn Indian blood," my mom would often holler in a fit of rage. One of the few memories I recalled from my youth. His "Indian blood' referred to his innate love of alcohol, non-committal wandering tendencies, and lack of fatherly care or child support for his only daughter. My parents had met in Sedona, Arizona while pursuing a spiritual quest. They spent weeks hiking canyons surrounding mystical red rock formations. A few years later she relocated with me in tow to Vegas while he took refuge at the pueblo.

The outside line where my inner thigh touched my bathing suit looked scarlet contrasted against my wheat colored pubic area. For relief, I walked back beside Luke in the shade.

"Good idea, you don't want to burn too early in the trip." He said, turning to me with a smile.

His concern and sexy grin warmed my core, feeling almost as crimson as my bikini line. "Have you ever participated in a ritual?"

"Is fishing a ritual?"

I giggled. "Maybe to you, but no. More like a religious ritual."

"Just church every Sunday with my step-mom, until my teenage years. That's a ritual, right? Why do you ask?"

"I thought about the idol and some rituals I saw in Africa and among Pueblo tribes. I'm trying to think of a commonality in the different ceremonies."

"Do you think they're related?"

I searched my mind, "I think they are all used to create order." I finished my beer in one gulp. "I need to use the ladies room. Can you slow down please?"

He idled the engines and I hovered off the stern just above the water. A random wave hit the port side of the Intrepid, instantly jolting my body sideways. I grabbed the rail, and felt my hand slip. Falling overboard seemed inevitable.

"Shit," I yelled just before hitting the water.

I gasped, held my breath and tumbled underwater, my heart racing with panic. I tumbled deeper and deeper, unable to react. I couldn't breathe, and my mind flashbacked to when I was a child caught in a rip current. I was helpless then, but not now. I unraveled my legs and started kicking. I soon realized I was under the boat. I could see the engines, and started kicking my feet away from them, my arms propelling me through the water. Desperate for air, I wanted to suck in a breath, but I knew water entering my lungs would cause me to panic even more.

"Raves." I heard Lucas holler. "Raves."

I surfaced, still kicking my feet to stay afloat. "Lucas, help." He stood at the side of the boat, dangling a life jacket.

"Grab the other end of the jacket. I'll pull you to the back of the boat."

I held one end until I felt the boat's platform.

"The ladder is under the platform. Just flip it down."

After climbing aboard, I finally inhaled a calming breath. "That wave came from nowhere. I was holding on tight, but, it was powerful."

He held my waist, "Are you okay?"

"Yes, just freaked out. You know the memory I have nearly drowning as a kid. I'm just not comfortable being alone in the water."

"You handled it well. I had you in sight within seconds of you going over. You swam away from the boat and then surfaced near the side."

He stared at me for a moment while I caught my breath.

25

"You probably need one of these." He handed me a cold beer. "I watched someone drown once. I was young and I couldn't do a thing. I remember it clearly, and if I felt like you were in great danger I would've rescued you. I didn't dive in because I wanted you to gain a bit of confidence in the water."

I wrapped myself in a towel. "I can think of less terrifying ways to become a better swimmer."

"You'll be an expert by the end of our trip," he said with a mischievous grin.

CHAPTER THREE

BENIN, AFRICA. 1714

Ebo emerged from his hut at the crack of dawn. After lighting the cooking fire, he walked to the nearby ocean to hopefully net some fish. The smell of burnt wood filled the damp morning air. Glancing at the sea, he immediately noticed a large ship in the distance. It was only the second time he had seen the foreign beast, but he knew it meant bloodshed. When he filled a bucket full of small fish, he returned to his home.

His wife, Yuwa finished breakfast preparations just as he reappeared. Her protruding belly was barely noticeable on her tall, thin frame, even at six months pregnant. She handed him a plate of mushy manioc with fish sauce.

"The foreign ship has returned," he said with concern. "We need enough water and food for a few days." He scooped a handful of food into his mouth. "I'll make a quick trip to the village."

Ebo had dark skin, a white, contagious smile and a warm heart. As the only surviving son in his family, he inherited an acre of farm land when his parents passed away two years ago.

Of Fon decent, he was very aware of the expansion of the Dahomey kingdom into his birth land. His people were being shipped off in chains to work aboard ships sailing to foreign lands. He wanted to remain unnoticed and keep his family safe. Any resistance to the neighboring tribe or the foreigners would instantly result in the slaughter of his family and loss of his precious land. He could trade some of his fresh fish he caught this morning for some much needed grain.

He handed Yuwa a piece driftwood he found at the beach. "This is not for fire," he said with an intense stare. "It has a powerful stone within, so I'm going to carve it as an offering for Agwe. I do not think it is of this world."

His wife placed the thick log in the corner of their hut. Made of solid mahogany, it looked perfectly round in the center at one end and bluntly flat on the other. It appeared phallic, enigmatically designed by nature. At the rounded end, deep in the center sat a rose crystal, barely visible.

Ebo returned hours later with one bucket filled with rice and millet and one full of water. "We need to use the water sparingly," he said. "The warriors are invading the village, and many of our people have been captured." He placed the buckets outside their mud shelter. "The kingdom is becoming corrupt, and our people are being traded for firearms, rum and tobacco."

"I prayed to the ancestors for your safe return," Yuwa said.

Ebo spent the rest of the day whittling the wood with his small iron carving knife. He started forming the head around the crystal, hollowing out and shaping his eyes, ears, lips and nose. Next he created his chest, waist, bent arms and sturdy legs. The flat base remained as the idol's platform. He detailed the statue's features by shaping his genitals, hands, feet and hair. He carved a hole in its left hand, and crafted a sword from a smaller scrap of wood.

"I have a warrior to offer to Agwe, the spirit of the sea tomorrow, so he will protect us from the evils of the foreign ship."

"I do not think it is safe." Yuwa begged.

It was dark when Ebo woke, the sun just beginning to show the faint light of dawn. He walked a little over a mile along a narrow trail to the water's edge, carrying his idol, a white candle and a small torch. He lit the candle with the flame. Following Vodun tradition, he took a handful of water, placing a drop of water to the right of the candle, one in the center and one to the left. He first addressed the main god. "Papa Legba, I ask for protection for my home and family." He held up the statue, "Agwe, I offer you this warrior I carved, which holds a powerful crystal. It came from the sea and should be returned to it." He glanced at the large vessel in the distance. "I ask for protection against the foreigners. To guard me, my family and village from…"

Two men grabbed him from behind, he dropped his present to the spirit of the sea onto the sand. "Thou shall not worship foreign idols." A third said, picking up the idol. He wore a loose ruffled shirt, tan trousers, a pigtail half-way down his back and a three-cornered blue hat. "Take him to the ship."

They shackled Ebo's wrists and tossed him into a canoe full of other young men bound in chains. They loaded the French frigate with human cargo, finished their final preparations, and set sail for the transatlantic crossing to the New World. The slaves would disembark in Haiti, the frigate and its crew would then sail to Cuba.

As the ship departed it was surrounded by a greenish glow.

CHAPTER FOUR

MAY 27, 2011

NASSAU, BAHAMAS

Nassau is the densely inhabited capital of the Bahamas, and not as naturally beautiful as the other islands in the chain, at least not in its current overdeveloped state. We pulled into a massive tourist resort on Paradise Island appropriately named Atlantis. The salmon colored buildings rose above the island as if the city itself emerged from the sea. Enormous gates and seahorses flanked the entryway as I gawked in awe at its cyclopean presence. Our boat seemed like a Kayak in comparison to countless mega-yachts lining the marina. I felt like a midget entering the land of giants, the feeling intensified by the contrast of hours at sea with nothing substantial on the horizon until now.

I rubbed my eyes, and joined Lucas at the helm, standing with his bare chest puffed out like a rooster. "Wow, this is where we meet up with the big boat?" I asked.

"Well not as big as these," he said looking around. "I need to find the dock master to get a slip. Then we'll look for Nick and Jamie."

He spotted a man in uniform walking towards us and called out, "Hey boss, I need a slip for the night."

The dock master waved him forward a few hundred feet and pointed to a slip between two similar sized craft. He helped tie the lines, then disappeared.

After securing our Intrepid we meandered through a maze of yachts. "So what's the name of the Bluewater?" I asked following slightly behind.

Slowing his pace, he said "It's named *Cabin Fever.*"

"Cute," I mumbled. Checking out boat names I noticed a rather large ship called *Sea-Licious,* followed by *Fantasea, Ashore Bet, Reel Busy, Finale, Miss Fitz* and a mid-sized boat called *What's Up Dock.*

How clever, I thought. Boat owners seemed inventive in choosing names, probably selecting one reflecting their occupation, personality or pleasures. Passing a boat called *O-Sea-D,* I realized such a name revealed something too personal to the general public. Creative yes, but a bit of oversharing. Our choice name for the Intrepid, *Breakfast in Bimini,* seemed sophisticated and unique in comparison.

We approached the stern of *Cabin Fever* and Jamie jumped onto the dock, greeting by waving her hands high above her head. "Hey, you guys made it. How was the crossing?" Her voice was warm, strong, and slightly southern.

Before I could answer, she hugged me and then dashed to greet Lucas. Shortly after, we climbed aboard the Bluewater. I recognized Nick, who sat reading a book on the couch.

"Hey, you're here." A robust 6'2, he towered above me when he stood, and then bent down for a gentle embrace. Turning to Lucas he firmly shook his hand and patted him on the back. "So, you made good time with no problems along the way?"

Lucas snorted before retelling the submarine encounter while I moseyed over to help Jamie fix cocktails in the kitchen. Jamie also appeared statuesque, with a heathy solid build revealing curves where appropriate in her hips, full breasts, and a trim yet slight softness around her waist. Her pale skin, thin lips and shoulder length dark blonde hair reminded me of my German aunt.

Wine is good for the soul, my aunt used to tell me as a teenager, and now I couldn't agree more. *Hell, even beer and rum seemed good for the soul.*

"Do you need help?" I asked.

"Nope. I just made you two rum runners and refreshed mine." She handed me two drinks. "It's a traditional welcome drink."

32

I glanced at the drinks, then back at her questioningly.

"I didn't make them too strong," she said.

"It looks refreshing," I said, unintentionally licking my bottom lip.

Nick and Lucas were both laughing, so the two of us drifted over to join their conversation. I passed Lucas his drink, and silently listened to him recap the submarine incident. It suddenly became comical instead of the harrowing experience it seemed like just a few hours ago. I even giggled at myself for naively silencing the radio.

Jamie tapped her glass to mine, then touched it to the rim of the other two. "Here's to a fun and safe excursion. We picked up *Cabin Fever* in Miami three days ago, and came straight here." Walking into the galley and peering into the oven, she said, "I'm making some biscuits." She raised her hand toward the rear of the boat. "While they finish, let me show you two around."

Nick settled back into the couch. Lucas and I placed our drinks on the kitchen counter, then followed Jamie for a tour. "This is the master bedroom," she opened her arms wide. The bed looked ruffled and loosely made. "This is where Nick and I are sleeping over the next few weeks." Dressers flanked both sides of the bed and a door leading to a private bathroom nestled to the right. I peeked inside.

"It's small, but has the basics. Shower, toilet, sink," Jamie said, stepping past the foot of the bed to the back of the room. "And we have a door leading to the stern," she opened it and stepped out. Lucas followed as I stood peering out at the dock. "You can also access the stern from the either side of the boat, but feel free to come through our bedroom."

"Nice," I murmured while retreating, and allowing the others access into the petite room.

We wandered back towards the front stopping at a second door. "Here are your sleeping quarters for the next few weeks." Jamie slid open a door revealing a bed with a small dresser at its base. She extended her arm, "It's just a bed, but it's all you really need."

Lucas snickered while climbing onto the mattress, "It'll work." He stretched out as if sleeping, then jumped up, slapping my ass when Jamie turned towards the main cabin.

We strolled back to the galley where she glanced into the oven and turned it off. She opened several cabinets while pointing to random items, "Here we have coffee, snacks, drinks, canned goods, condiments. Help yourself."

Lucas chimed in, "We're going to the grocery soon to stock up on supplies." Grabbing his drink and taking a swig he asked, "Do you want to come with us, or can we get you anything?"

"I have a list, if you don't mind." She handed me a piece of paper. "It's just a few things."

I stuck it in my pocket, "No problem."

We continued our tour past the galley "Here's the main living area, TV and the dining table. The couch opens into a bed, but we won't need it." Following Jamie we passed Nick, who was once more engrossed in a book. She gestured forward, "This is the main bathroom."

A moment later she pointed to some controls just beneath the front windows, "The inside helm, of course." It stood out like an elephant at a tea party. Wheels, gears, and navigation gauges sat next to the plush couch, with a petite clouded window. You could barely see beyond the extended bow.

"Do you use it?" Lucas asked. "You can't really see much from here. Up top is the place to be while navigating."

"The upper deck is where we spend most of our time," she said. "This is really just in case the weather is really bad. We haven't used it yet, and I hope we don't need to." She chuckled. "Let's go see the bridge."

We walked out the side door and climbed about eight steps leading to the upper deck, the bridge. The 360 view of the harbor took my breath away, with mega-yachts as far as the eye could see and a pink Mayan Pyramid in the distance. I giggled. So somebody's idea of the lost city of Atlantis included the ancient Mayan culture.

"Why is there a huge Mayan pyramid in the middle of the resort?" I finally asked.

Both Jamie and Lucas glanced at me, harmoniously answering "It's a water slide. It's actually pretty fun and steep."

"Sounds cool," I mindlessly responded, checking out the rest of the upper deck. It was completely open with the exception of a soft canvas top covering the helm, captain's chair and two rectangular seats. Transparent rolls of vinyl were slightly hanging and snapped to the canvas. Isinglass, I recalled from our boat, used to shelter the occupants from wind and water during rough seas or thunderstorms. My eyes scanned the rest of the deck, mentally noting the abundance of sunbathing space on couches situated around the outer rim.

Lucas interrupted my thoughts, "Hey honey, are you ready to go grocery shopping?"

Always, I thought but answered, "Yes, let's go."

We returned to the galley and polished off our drinks.

Lucas confirmed directions to the grocery store. "About a ten minute walk?"

"Yes. And we're well stocked on vodka, rum, wine, beer and mixers. Priorities." She smiled.

I truly enjoyed grocery shopping in foreign countries and browsing different products. It seemed more adventurous than tedious overseas, an enthusiasm I didn't have while visiting the superstores in the states.

We darted through pedestrian and automotive traffic, and ten minutes later arrived at City Market slightly sweaty. The Atlantis resort dominated the block. We spotted the market across from the main entrance, tucked in between several high end retail shops.

In the store, I pulled Jamie's list from my pocket and glanced at the items. Lemons, wasabi paste, soy sauce, kidney beans, coconut milk, yogurt, lettuce, tomatoes, green and jalapeno peppers. I had a general list of other items we needed in my head.

We returned to the *Cabin Fever*, arms loaded with plastic bags. Jamie immediately started putting things away while Nick continued to read.

"I'm going to our boat to get luggage and supplies." Lucas announced.

"Wax beans?" Jamie asked, raising her eyebrows.

"I'd like to make a bean salad at some point. It's full of protein and pretty tasty." I grabbed the spices and jams, placing them in the cupboard. "I bought guava jam."

"That would be good with baked Brie," she said.

"Damn, I didn't buy any Brie. Should I go back?"

"I have some."

"Sweet. I'm going to help Lucas, unless you need my help?" I asked, glancing at the one remaining bag.

"No, you go. I'm fine."

Meandering through the marina I questioned my ability to

relocate the Intrepid. I remembered docking near two smaller boats, so I looked for a threesome pattern and headed in the direction of the closest grouping. I stumbled upon our luggage sitting on the dock, and spotted Lucas on *Breakfast in Bimini*.

Good thinking, I congratulated myself, "Hey, sweetie. Did you have trouble finding the boat?"

He glimpsed up wryly, "I looked at the slip number when we docked."

"Smartass." I silently mumbled and then more loudly, "Oh, makes sense. What can I do?"

"The garbage bin is at the end of the dock," he said, handing me a beer box filled with empty bottles.

I strolled to the bin, then back to where the cooler and statue now lay next to our luggage. A quick glimpse into the ice box holding fresh caught dolphin, cleaned and bagged with a few pieces of ice still floating around, reminded me of the bloodbath just a few hours prior. I picked up the statue, dropping it onto my bag. It radiated an intense heat, almost burning my hand.

"Damn." I heard myself sharply say, "Stupid idol."

Lucas didn't acknowledge my outburst, but continued scrubbing, and then spraying the sides, deck and engines of the Intrepid. Two teenaged girls in drenched bathing suits ran by giggling. The air smelled of greasy hamburgers, and I glanced around looking for the source of the tempting smell. Four boats over I noticed a 100 foot Viking, smoke billowing from a grill on the stern as a handful of kids sat at a round table, squirting ketchup and mustard on their burgers. It smelled so good, although I didn't eat red meat my stomach rumbled. I realized the only thing I'd eaten all day was a piece of toast.

Lucas looked up, sweat dripping from his forehead to the dock. "Those burgers sure smell good."

"Yes they do. Jamie stocked up on hamburger meat and veggie burgers if we want some for lunch."

"Yeah. I'm done here," he said, turning off the water and putting away the hose. He lifted the cooler and a backpack, "Can you grab the other bags please."

I mindfully unzipped my duffel and pushed the statue inside with the backside of my hand. It didn't feel as hot. Could the sun warm wood that much? And how did it cool so quickly? I found myself falling behind and hurried to catch up.

Arriving at *Cabin Fever*, we found Nick and Jamie in the living room reviewing navigation maps while snacking on biscuits stuffed with Brie and guava jam. Lucas dropped the cooler on the dock while I set our luggage on our petite bed, then joined everyone else hovering over the charts.

Nick pointed to a section of the map, "This is our problem area tomorrow. It's called the Yellow Bank, and we need plenty of sunlight to read the waters." He peered at Lucas, "We literally will be dodging coral heads."

My eyes widened, but I kept quiet.

"Now, we know the general area of where they are, but it's impossible to map their exact location." He placed his fingertips together. "What we have going for us is the view from the bridge and hopefully plenty of sunlight. Once we're past there, it's smooth sailing."

"What if we don't have sunlight?" I shot back. The three stared at me.

"Never mind, just asking," I said.

"We'll leave at sunrise. Lucas, you follow me in the Intrepid and we'll tie your boat to ours at the fuel dock." Nick reached for a loaded biscuit, and the rest of us mimicked his move.

"Will do," Lucas replied as he finished his biscuit in two bites and reached for another.

I did the same but took six bites to finish the snack, then whispered, "Let's forget the burgers. These biscuits are amazing and filling."

He held up his finger, "Speaking of ..." He disappeared outside, then returned with the cooler. "Do you guys want mahi-mahi tonight?" He handed two large bags to Jamie.

"Oh yeah, I have the perfect marinade for this." She immediately started prepping the fish, grabbing spices and sauces, effortlessly dancing around the galley with the fish as her partner.

Lucas urged me to bring out my statue. After organizing my clothes, I reappeared, holding it up proudly, "Look what I found on the beach in Bimini."

Swapping the statue for a rum runner and waiting for Jamie's response, I finally got, "Uga-Bugga. I think you should name it Uga-Bugga."

Stifling a giggle, I almost spit out my drink mid-sip. Jamie handed the statue to Nick who examined it. "This is an interesting

37

piece," he said while rotating the idol. "It appears handmade, with a strange hole at the top of its head and at the back of the leg." I listened intently as the other two lost interest. "The eyes are carved out like they could have held stones, or at least its right eye. The left is a bit narrow. I've never seen anything like it. It certainly doesn't look Bahamian."

He contemplated it, then handed it back.

I peered into its eyes. "Maybe an emerald?" I wondered aloud. "I think it's unique and I'm on a quest to find its origin. My gut feeling suggests Africa, but I have no evidence yet." I shifted my gaze from the idol to Nick, "I just hope it doesn't have any bad omens or anything weird. It radiates a strange energy, a glow, and even heat sometimes."

He smirked, "Sounds like your imagination. Unless it proves otherwise, I'll leave it at just a statue."

***

After an excellent fish dinner complete with rice and beans, I put on one of the few dresses I packed for an evening adventure into the Atlantis resort and casino. Enormous columns imitating the Egyptian temples of Luxor flanked the foyer. I started feeding one of the machines quarters. Lucas touched my right elbow and murmured, "Let's check out the aquarium first, then we can play."

"I didn't know they had an aquarium." I followed his lead down the stairs past several contemporary restaurants arriving at a colossal glass window housing what appeared to be the entire Atlantic Ocean. Soft serene music played in the background as schools of fish floated before my eyes. "This is beautiful."

"Oh, but there's more." He muttered and gestured to his left. "The main entrance is over here."

I stared in awe at the marine life, not wanting to move just yet. Pale grey fish with yellow tails swam by, along with tiny yellow fish with blue eyes and colorful rainbow fish with hints of pink, turquoise and green. A shadow suddenly filled the aquarium as my head and eyes tilted upward. I pointed to the top of the window at a huge ray drifting there. "Wow. I've never seen such a large stingray."

"It's a Manta Ray," Lucas said.

The manta glided through the water with the grace of an eagle riding mountain thermals, effortless and timeless. I half expected Chopin's "Tristesse" to start playing in the background as angels appeared above. The classical music played in my head as the manta turned toward me with a large, elegant smile the size of my entire body. I beamed back. A remora hovered around its large triangular wings, minuscule in comparison.

Lucas took my hand, gently leading me into the main entry where a Mayan archaeological theme jolted me out of the natural magical beauty into fantasy land.

"Where does this Atlantis Mayan connection come from? The Mayans in Mexico have nothing to do with Plato's Atlantis. They're two different parts of the world, completely separate cultures. Not to mention…"

Lucas interrupted my tirade, "Honey, it's just a resort. Don't overanalyze."

"You're right," I sighed.

We passed several small tanks housing seahorses and the perpetually graceful jellyfish, artificially lit up and pulsating bright neon pink. Stopping to admire them for a moment, we continued to the next exhibit, a glass tunnel. Marine life surrounded us as if we were submerged. A shark glided overhead, and then to eye level. Tuna, grouper, stingrays, sharks and the distant eel peacefully co-existed.

"Don't they want to eat each other?" I asked with concern.

He glanced at me sideways. "I think they feed them."

"But still it's their instinct. I mean a shark with a tuna, in the marina they go nuts for tuna scraps."

He shrugged, "I don't know."

We strolled through the lobster tunnel where thousands of them lay overhead and on each side of the passageway. Nasty looking creatures, but tasty.

We moved into another room scattered with ruins and artifacts of mixed cultures. In one tank sat a statue of Poseidon raising his trident in the air. I snickered, my eyes lingering on the image longer than I expected. I pulled myself away and sashayed over to Lucas gazing at a container full of small flat silver fish.

"What are these?" I asked.

"Piranhas."

I gasped while leaning in and examining their mouths. A bulbous head with big razor sharp teeth gazed back at me. I cringed. "I'm glad they're not in the Atlantic waters, only in South American rivers, the Amazon and such."

He laughed. "Yeah, that'd be a challenge while swimming."

Opposite the piranhas sat an exhibit lined with fake ceramic vases and jars housing moray eels. They also exposed sharp teeth, a big green slimy head and blue beady eyes with pottery jars concealing their bodies.

This must be the scary flesh-eating room, I thought, scurrying after Lucas as he headed for the exit.

I caught up to him in the lobby, "Let's get a drink and then hit the casino," he suggested.

We climbed the stairs to the entrance, coming across a bar where Lucas ordered me a glass of Pinot Grigio and himself vodka and cranberry with a splash of tonic. I took a long sip from my wine, as we walked into the brightly lit room. "So, what's your game for the night?"

"Poker."

The casino was noisy, with slots screaming various mechanical chants. A machine singing, "Wheel of Fortune" caught my attention.

"I'm feeling good vibes from this machine." I said, sitting down and feeding it a $100 bill.

"I'll be at the tables over there, honey." He pointed to a roped off area in the center of the room.

Within fifteen minutes I lost the $100. I realized my intuition must be off.

The familiar sound of coins hitting steel was missing in this casino. When I was a kid, my mom worked at the Las Vegas Flamingo as a dealer. Although I didn't spend much time there as a child, when she'd pick up her check or visit the casino she often gave me a roll of quarters. Back then nobody really paid attention to a kid playing slots. Credits and tickets had replaced the coins, and I found it less exciting.

I stopped by the poker area to check on Lucas. "Hey sweetie, do you need anything?" I asked.

"No, they've been taking care of me." He glanced at his cards, making a pass hand signal to the dealer.

I stumbled upon a brilliant glass sculpture, recognizing the work of Dale Chihuly, a sculptor known for his statues at the Bellagio in Las Vegas. It radiated heat with red, yellow and orange glass entwined resembling Medusa on fire. It drew me in. I could feel its heat, causing beads of sweat to form on my forehead. It kept me mesmerized for a few breathless moments.

A roar from a nearby slot machine broke my trance. It depicted a cartoon of an angry looking Poseidon holding a trident and riding a barnacled humpback whale. Wanting to receive good fortune from the god of the sea, I put a $20 bill in the machine and pushed the maximum bet. Various images of tridents, Poseidon, sea monsters and a wild card spun around a single line on the dollar machine, with three identical ones on the center line needed for a win. The wild card could substitute for any of the symbols at maximum bet. I watched my credits dwindle. Two images of Poseidon and a wild card lined up. I waited for the credits to pour in, but nothing. "What the hell." I looked around for an attendant.

I felt a light touch on my right arm and glanced back to find Lucas. "This should be a win. I pushed max bet."

He looked at the displayed bet amount. "It only shows you bet two credits."

I let out a long frustrating grunt. "I must have run out of money. I definitely pushed the max button as I always do, I just didn't check the amount. I should have won $300. I guess the god of the sea wasn't looking out for me."

"Same here, I lost a few hundred. That's unusual for me. Are you ready to head back?"

On the way out, I spotted another glass sculpture perched atop a temple. Contrary to the heated Chihuly monument, this one looked cool and calm, emanating a yin presence. Cobalt blue mottled with opalescent white glass. The moon, I imagined. A vibrant carpet lay beneath the temple and constellations painted on the ceiling framed the piece. I spotted an image of Poseidon among the stars. He seemed to be omnipresent this evening, but not in a favorable way.

When we arrived at the yacht, Nick and Jamie were snuggled on the couch watching a movie. We fixed another drink and shared our Atlantis experience with them, and then retreated to our sleeping quarters.

I was jolted awake in the middle of the night with a light finger sliding down the bottom of my right foot. A chill fluttered through my entire body, leaving me breathless and frightened. I glanced over at Lucas snoring.

What the hell? I'd thought I'd been dreaming, but I knew what I felt was real. My heart raced. A gloomy voice whispered I opened a portal. What kind of portal? The voice and finger running down my foot seemed so realistic and creepy. I sat up, attempting to slow my breath and calm my pounding heart.

I wasn't alone here. Lucas slept by my side and as far as I could tell we were still in the marina.

Breathe slow, I repeated to myself while snuggling closer to my love, my protector.

CHAPTER FIVE

MAY 28, 2011

NASSAU TO NORMANS

With the boat rocking, and the sun rising I glanced out the window and noticed we were moving. I threw on my jean shorts and a tank top, and then slowly wandered into the main cabin, finding my sea legs along the way.

The seas must be rough, I realized. Stumbling through the galley, I found a mug and helped myself to a warm pot of brewed coffee. I peered through the sliders, blinking in the morning light, and spotted Lucas on our boat maneuvering next to *Cabin Fever*. He looked a bit stressed, yelling commands and throwing lines towards the big boat. Not wanting to disturb anyone, I gingerly climbed to the bridge with a half cup of coffee and sat in silence next to Jamie at the helm. The guys worked on securing our smaller boat to the Bluewater.

"Damn weatherman!" Lucas said, climbing back aboard the big boat. "Calm, my ass. It's blowing like crazy. They always get it wrong." He was a serious man when it came to weather, studying it from every angle. He could have easily been a meteorologist, but he once told me he didn't like working on someone else's schedule.

He noticed me sitting near the helm and called up, "Good

morning sunshine. Did you enjoy your extra time sleeping in?"

Is he being sarcastic? Uncertain, I smiled and answered "Yes sweetie, thanks."

Jamie turned towards me and whispered, "We've only been on the move for about a half hour, that's not really sleeping in."

"I thought he would have woken me."

"No need," she quickly responded. "We have it totally under control. We are fueled up, the boats are tethered and we are on our way."

"But a bit rough?" I asked.

"More than predicted or ideal, but we'll make do."

Nick and Lucas joined us, both strongly suggesting getting everything in the cabin secured for a rough ride while we still had a bit of protection near land, and to prepare some sandwiches and snacks for later in the day.

I followed Jamie and asked, "What do I need to do?"

"First, make sure everything in your room is on the floor or put away. Then start on the sandwiches," she urged.

Reaching our bedroom, I placed the few things on the floor, and then hurried to the galley and pulled out all the makings for sandwiches. "Do you guys like mayo?" I asked Jamie, who vigorously moved things about in the living room.

"Yes. Mayo is great," she answered.

I made two peanut butter and jelly, four baloney and ham with cheese and four turkey and cheese sandwiches. I stuffed them into the empty sack from the loaf and secured everything I could in the galley. Spotting the paper plates on the counter I snagged a few and placed the rest in a cabinet. I double checked the cupboard latches to make sure they were all hooked.

Jamie looked up at me and sighed, "Okay, let's go to the bridge and hope for the best."

"Should I bring the sandwiches?"

"Yes. We can put them in the small refrigerator up there with the drinks." She pointed at the sliders while moving her index finger back and forth, "It's not a great idea to be going up and down those stairs if it gets really rough." She laughed nervously and continued, "Especially if you're not used to boating."

My eyes widened, "I forgot something in my room," I mumbled dashing towards the bedroom. I reached over the statue lying on the floor and grabbed a full pack of cigarettes and a lighter from my backpack. Lucas had some on the bridge, but I didn't want to run out and be smokeless during a turbulent trip. My eyes skimmed the idol as memories of the dream about the portal flashed through my mind. Such a vivid vision of the finger scraping my foot followed by the low whisper, "you opened a portal." I cringed, but hurried out the door.

"I'm ready, just needed some smokes. I had a dream last night I'll tell you about later."

She ignored my comment and warned me to use the rail as we climbed to the bridge. The boat steadily rocked side to side.

Once on the upper deck, I stashed the bag in a thigh high fridge and felt my way to an oblong cushion across from the boys navigating. Nick steered the vessel while peering into the distance and Lucas stood next to him examining charts. I never considered Lucas to be a small guy, in fact I'd consider him husky, but with Nick towering over him he looked small. Jamie took a seat next to me. We sat in silence, watching the land disappear as the sun radiated above. At barely 8:00 a.m., the heat was already intense and with cumulus clouds building around us the humidity felt extreme.

"We have about 45 nautical miles to go and at just under ten knots an hour," Nick called out, "We should arrive at Norman's in about five hours. I just hope we can avoid these storms because we certainly can't outrun them." He gestured at the sky before turning his attention forward.

I glanced at Jamie looking for a response, or a sign of what to expect. Perhaps I needed an optimistic smile or a pep talk.

Shouldn't we just wait for better sea conditions? I thought. *Another night in Nassau would be okay.*

"As long as we stay out of lightning we'll be fine." Lucas said.

The boat rolled more heavily and visions of lighting cracking around us flooded my mind. Panic took over, and I must have turned white because Jamie placed her hand on my shoulder and said, *Cabin Fever* is a wonderful boat. It's just a little rough, you'll get used to it. We are fine Raves."

I swallowed and nervously started shaking my left leg. "So maybe we should stay in Nassau and wait for a better day to cruise," I said, glancing back at the disappearing island.

"Today is as good as any other," she said, changing the subject. "So you lived in California?"

I nodded. "Grew up in Vegas and moved to San Pedro as a teenager. I liked both places, California a bit more. I guess because of my age, and my mom being happily married. I felt like I had a family for the first time."

"You didn't boat much in San Pedro? Isn't there a harbor nearby?"

"Yeah, I loved the harbor. I'd rollerblade there and watch the ships come in." I felt myself relax at the memory. "Boating wasn't really a part of my life then. I admired the ocean from ashore. Besides the water is much colder than Florida or the Bahamas. I've been on boats for short rides, Long Beach to Catalina for example. And I had a really rough ride in Indonesia while taking a boat to see Komodo Dragons."

I beamed, reminiscing about my travels. Jamie seemed attentive. "Water sprayed everywhere, soaking us as we bounced up and down and back and forth." I giggled. "But you know I was young and carefree. Once we got there, the Komodo Dragons were something to see. We just walked past a few and I asked if they were man-eaters." My grin widened. "Yeah," the guide said. "But the old ones won't hurt you. Then we saw them feeding, and what a frenzy--"

The bow of the boat slammed into the Atlantic as Nick yelled, "Hold-on." *Cabin Fever* leaned violently to the right then to the left as the refrigerator broke free, skidding across the deck. I paled and grimaced. Lucas carefully retrieved the fridge, it seemed intact and upright. He bungeed it back to the railing.

"Be careful," I hollered. "Do you need help?" As if I could do anything.

"Nope. It's under control." He shouted back lighting a cigarette.

Damn, I could use a drag right now. As the Kramers were non-smokers, we agreed only to smoke on the back of the Bluewater, using a water bottle for an ashtray. A cigarette should have been the last thing on my mind, but I needed one.

"I'm going to join my honey for a smoke." I told Jamie. "Do you mind?"

"No problem. Just take it slow and steady. We wouldn't want to lose you out here," she said matter-of-factly.

My eyes widened as I second guessed my decision. The nicotine craving won, and I made my way along the deck like a centipede.

Lucas looked at me incredulously. "You don't need to crawl, honey. Just walk carefully."

"I don't want to smash against the rail like the fridge," I shot back as I reached him. "Hold me so I can have a cig please?" He lit one handing it to me as I snuggled between his knees.

Looking behind and to my right, I saw nothing but white caps on the chaotic ocean, and towering dark clouds above. Our Intrepid bopped around like a kangaroo behind us. In the distance a blue-grey shaft extended from the sky to sea. I pointed in the direction of the shaft. "There's rain over there. Do you think it will get us?"

"Hard to say. I can't tell which way it's moving." He placed his cigarette butt in the semi-empty water bottle. "My main concern is the Yellow Bank. We have about an hour until we start crossing the corals. We need sunlight. Out here if it rains we get wet, no big deal unless lighting is around. Then, it's a completely different story."

My eyes widened as I took a drag from my cigarette, then dropped it into the water bottle. "Isn't it equipped with protection like the static wicks on the Cessna?"

He snickered. "This boat supposedly has a basic lightning protection system, but I don't trust it. One strike could knock out all the electronics, put a hole in the boat or even harm one of us."

Oh is that it, I thought but answered, "Why don't you trust it?"

"All metal in the boat is bonded together through an eight-gauge wire to a grounding block in the bottom of the hull where it terminates. Metal includes the engine, appliances, railings and so forth. If we're struck by lightning, its energy is dispersed through the boat to the water." He paused for reflection. "That's in theory. These systems are very unreliable and since this is a rental, even more so. They probably have it for insurance purposes, but I don't know how diligent this company is."

He stood up, stumbling slightly to the right, firmly reaching out his hand to mine. "Let's join Jamie and Nick. You don't need to crawl back, just hold onto me."

I grabbed his hand and with an unsteady stagger we made our way back to the helm. Jamie glanced up from the charts she studied. "Looks like you're an old pro walking back."

"Well, not quite," I chuckled. "But I learn quickly." I took a seat next to her and glanced at the maps splayed across her lap. "You seem very comfortable boating," I said with a slight rise in my voice.

"I grew up around boats. Lake boats, river boats, ocean yachts. My father loved fishing, and most of our holidays revolved around the water. I've lived most of my life in Corpus Christi, Texas. We'd spend weekends fishing in the Gulf of Mexico. Then in the summers we'd pick a lake for a two week vacation, Lake Michigan, Lake Erie, or Cumberland. We even spent a summer in Alaska on Iliamna Lake fishing for trout. We'd usually rent houseboats and stay aboard." Her slight smile broadened. "When I met Nick, I found he was just as experienced. Well, at least he thinks so," she whispered. "I taught him a lot. He used to have a captain do everything for him." She chuckled and raised her voice. "But now, he is the best captain I know." She winked at me.

Nick glanced our way. "Tell me tonight after I get us through this mess. And hand Lucas the charts, since he's my navigator."

Jamie reached over her husband, handing over the paper maps as Nick fussed with the GPS on the console. He zoomed into the Yellow Bank revealing our distance, speed and depth. Radar images overlapped the GPS displaying small green and yellow blemishes moving in a northwest direction.

"God damn weather," Nick muttered.

Lucas fixated on folding the maps to expose the Yellow Bank as they consulted each other.

The sun disappeared, the wind picked up, and the air filled with the pungent scent of rain. I remained silent.

Shit, we need sunlight, they'd said. Seconds later a light drizzle dampened *Cabin Fever* as I looked around for leadership. *I'm ready. Just tell me what to do. Bring it on,* my thoughts dared as my body seemed paralyzed.

We're fine, I silently repeated. *We have excellent captains and we're fine.*

The guys were discussing routes and weather and Jamie moved over to help troubleshoot. I watched intently.

This is why I asked about no sunlight prior to leaving. I guess we could slow down the boat or find another route around the shallow bank. But what do I know, I'm a nautical novice. Trust the experienced navigators, I concluded.

Nick throttled back, slowing our speed slightly.

"Here's the plan," Nick said with authority. "We have light, not direct sunlight, but we can still see the water. I need all eyes on the water while I watch the GPS. Lucas I need you to help guide between what you see on the charts with depths and what you see out there."

He turned towards me. "Raven I need you on the bow. Shout if you see coral heads or large dark spots. Call out their location as you would as if looking at the hands on a clock. 1:00, 2:00 et cetera."

He spun in Jamie's direction. "Jamie, you know what to do, be diligent with your water observations."

His eyes darted between the three of us. "It's not an ideal situation to be towing a thirty-six-foot boat through this shallow area in these seas, but I think it's our best option. I need Lucas here with me, not on the Intrepid." Nick slackened slightly. "The good news is it will take less than an hour to cross the bank."

We scattered like panicked mice. I cautiously made my way along the rail to the bow, ignoring the light pulsating rain. I stood firmly scanning the water intently. Jamie stood to my right, so I covered more of the left hemisphere and center glancing to the right from time to time. I adapted to the side-to-side sway, but every few minutes the bow dramatically pitched forward. Each time I clenched the rail so tight my hands turned pale, my body occasionally dropping to a squat while still gripping firmly. I noticed a large grey spot, its position and relevance probably not a concern on our present heading.

I called out to Jamie just in case, "There's a dark spot at my 10:00."

She joined me at the rail as I pointed.

"It's a coral, but not in our path. That's exactly what we're looking for though, so good job." She scooted back to her previous post. A short time later she turned towards the cockpit and shouted, "Coral at our 12:30." Lucas, now shirtless, appeared at the bow next to Jamie. He returned to the helm and our course shifted left slightly.

Rain beaded on my face, arms and legs. I sporadically wiped my face with my hand in an attempt to spread the dampness and keep the water away from my eyes. My thick hair was damp but not soaked, and tied up in a pony-tail turned messy top-knot bun to keep it out of my face. I clasped the rail tightly since the pitch and yaw kept my adrenaline flowing and my gut clenched. With the turbulent sea, it surprised me more saltwater didn't come over the bow, but then again we were two stories above the waves. I scanned the bank and noticed corals in the distance, with one actually protruding from the water a few feet, but nothing in our direct path.

I briefly glanced back at the guys, who seemed busy talking and looking around the cockpit. Lucas pointed to the sky a few times and I looked up and saw darker clouds to our south. Jamie stood erect examining the sea. She glanced over at me and smiled. "Is everything okay?"

"Yeah. I'm fine," I beamed back just as the boat lurched forward and I quickly crouched.

"You'll get used to it. You're doing great," she shouted through her smile. She turned back around to study the surrounding water.

I peered more closely ahead and noticed a dark spot. I shouted, "Coral at my 11...ish." Jamie came over followed closely by Lucas quickly taking a peek and returning to the cockpit. Jamie lightly patted me on the back and returned to her post. *Cabin Fever* shifted slightly right of our current course.

I felt our speed increase. I figured we were more than halfway through the Yellow Bank and the boys were probably getting restless with an approaching storm.

"How does it look out there?" Nick shouted.

"Our path looks good at the moment," Jamie hollered.

"Same here," I concurred. My words were followed by a thunderous roar.

I anxiously glanced back at Lucas, who looked frightened. Jamie gave me a fleeting look, then turned towards Nick. "We'll stay here until you tell us otherwise," she shouted.

We will? I silently questioned. *What about us being the only vessel in the region?* Lightning is attracted to the highest object in an area, and the protection system might not work.

"Keep diligent," Nick shouted. "We're almost through, and we just need to stay focused."

I got flustered. Where there's thunder there's lightning. If lightning started to flash around us wouldn't we be better off in the cabin? We'd be better protected there...we'd have to be. I think Lucas just tried to freak me out earlier. Loss of electronics, holes in the boat, possible sinking. I didn't even give lightning a second thought prior to his explanation. The sky appeared darker, but I could still see the changes in depth and water color. I pointed to my 12:00 and shouted "Coral?"

She peered uncertainly at a dark spot, calling out, "Lucas we may have something here at our twelve."

Appearing briefly Lucas sputtered, "Best to move left or right. Just in case." We veered slightly to the left as thunder roared. A flash of lightning momentarily blinded me followed by another angry drawn out rumble. The steady drizzle mutated into something akin to nails pounding my skin. The sea turned mad.

"Damn it." Screamed Nick. "Get back here ladies."

I cautiously found my way back to the cockpit, while Jamie did the same. Nick pulled back the throttle to a crawl and pointed to the radar. "We have a small red cell approaching, and as we just saw lightning. We need to move to the cabin, now."

Climbing down the stairs, I squeezed between Lucas and Nick as Jamie took the rear. Nick grabbed the inside controls, immediately taking the GPS cover off and powering up. I slid sideways, falling into the sliders and quickly finding a wall to lean against. The other two flanked Nick. A thin horizontal row of windows in front of the helm provided a view of the bow on a clear day, but with the pounding rain and the absence of windshield wipers they were useless. The Titanic could have crossed our path and we wouldn't have seen it. I had a better view from the side and kept my eyes on the water. A deafening boom made me jump and I saw Lucas cringe from the corner of my eye.

"That was close," he exclaimed.

"Talk about blind navigation," Nick quickly responded, rubbing the back of his neck. "We're doing five knots. I'm following the GPS, and hoping for the best. It's been pretty right-on through the bank." He stood firmly. "Are you doing okay back there Raves? I hope you're not leaning against metal?"

My eyes widened as another boom filled my ears. The boat rocked more violently in every direction. I glanced at the sliders, quickly realizing they had metal frames I stood and swayed to the left then right, catching myself before falling. I peeked at the other three, and saw them sway indifferently in unison, although Jamie stumbled backwards before she regained her balance. I backed up and used the granite kitchen counter to steady myself.

"I'm fine," I finally answered. Do you need me to do anything?" I hoped the answer would be "no" since I had a hard enough time just standing.

I heard plates grinding and shifting in the cupboard. Something fell, creating a thump in a distant bedroom. The ship rattled. Between the refrigerator, the shifting of items in the cabinets, the engine room or rails, I wondered if we hit a coral or was it just the rough seas tearing apart our ship as if it were a toy in a tempest.

"Just let me know if you see anything unusual through the sliders."

"Okay." I automatically responded. *If I see Atlantis rising from the sea, I'll definitely let you know. Otherwise, I can't really see much*, I thought.

After ten minutes, the pounding rain and thunder subsided. It seemed like a lifetime. The rocking eased a bit and my mind and body calmed.

"Lucas, can you take the controls for a minute then once I'm set on the bridge, check for any damage. Meet us there when you're done," Nick bellowed.

I followed the Kramers, leaving the sliding door slightly open for Lucas. The sky still looked dark on our port side, but sun rays to our right promised hope. I continued to scan the water in search of corals until told otherwise. I noticed the Intrepid swaying behind us. I let out a sigh of relief, surprised to see it still attached and floating. At the helm, the navigators examined the GPS and charts. I spotted a large dark coral head in the distance, but nowhere near our path.

Silence descended, not complete but a peaceful calm of ocean waves instead of pounding seas. There were no thunderous roars from the sky or Nick, just a steady rhythmic flow of nature. It wasn't flat by any means, just unobtrusive like the morning following Mardi Gras.

Nick finally called out, "We're clear of the Yellow Bank. Damn, talk about danger. The timing couldn't have been worse for the storm. I'm not sure if luck was on our side or not."

He turned towards me and asked, "Raven, can you hand me a beer and sandwich?"

I grabbed two cold beers from the small refrigerator, handing the guys each one. "What type of sandwich do you want? Baloney and ham, turkey or PB&J?"

"Turkey," Nick said.

"Baloney and ham for me," Lucas replied.

"I'll have turkey too," Jamie said, appearing by my side. A wide, thin lipped smile crossed her face. "I always get hungry after an adrenaline rush."

I chuckled while piling the sandwiches on plates, including a PB&J for myself and handed them out. I sat next to Jamie on a side cushion near the helm.

"I had a strange dream last night. I felt a fingernail slide down my foot and something whispered, 'you opened a portal.' It seemed so real and creepy," I told her.

Nick gave me a wry smile, then turned towards Lucas. "Are you whispering strange things in her ear at night?"

He laughed. "No, this is the first I've heard about this dream."

Nick pointed off the bow, "Normans is within view and no portal exists between us and our destination. It's just a strange dream."

"But it's the most vivid dream I've ever had," I said, defending myself.

"Honey, you have strange dreams all the time," Lucas said. "It probably has something to do with the statue you found and your active imagination."

"Humm," I murmured. Maybe it was all in my head, and I subconsciously picked up on something during the day, prompting the dream. But the nail scratch directly in the center of my foot was real. What if I somehow accidentally opened a portal?

CHAPTER SIX

MAY 28, 2011

NORMANS CAY

The navy water turned sheer topaz as we anchored off Norman's Cay. Lucas dove off the bow to set the anchor as Jamie followed with a whopping splash and immense holler.

"Woo-hoo." She waved her hands in the air, "Come on in Raves."

Dashing to the bottom deck for a less spectacular entrance, I shed my shirt and jumped feet first. Bobbing to the surface, Lucas grabbed my waist surprising me with a kiss on the lips.

"Yum. Salty," I said, kissing him more deeply.

Pulling my bathing suit bikini bottoms, he teased and tugged. I in turn pulled down his swimsuit. A struggle ensued as he tried to yank off my bikini with me giggling and wrestling to keep it.

Moments later Jamie emerged from the water next to us. "Children," she playfully scolded.

Lucas submerged, so I plunged underwater and took the opportunity to swim toward shore, to the best of my rudimentary ability. Arms flailing and feet kicking in the shallow water, I arrived out of breath. He caught me at the waterline, tickling my ribs. "Wait," I screamed and giggled, trying to break loose. "Look there's a duck," I pointed to my right.

He laughed and didn't stop.

"No, really. Look."

He smirked. I pointed to the duck rapidly moving back and forth gazing out to sea. It seemed stressed and anxious just staring at the ocean. I laughed with concern. "What's her problem?"

Lucas seemed undisturbed, refocusing his attention on Jamie and Nick swimming toward shore. I studied the bird as I rested on the powdery sand. Her nervous movements made me worried, and I wanted to join its pacing and help it discover a resolution to its problem. The nursery rhyme and game "duck, duck, goose," flooded my mind as childhood memories of the kindergarten pastime caused me to shiver.

I had very limited memories prior to age ten, leading me to believe I'd shut out painful events. But I recalled being picked as the goose and then chasing other kids in a circle around the room. *Why does a goose chase ducks? What a strange game.* I shook off my rare recollection.

"Is the anchor secure?" Nick asked, climbing out of the water.

"Yes. I buried it in the sand," Lucas said, standing up to meet him.

Jamie floated in the shallow water not yet wanting to emerge. "That's one neurotic duck," she called out.

I laughed and nodded with a quick response, "Yeah, it's making me anxious. Perhaps she needs a strong drink."

"Good idea, let's hit the beach club for a Goombay Smash, and then explore the island," Jamie suggested.

"I'm in," I said.

The four of us walked just fifty-feet from the beach to an open-air but screened-in restaurant and bar. Wooden steps flanked with palm trees, cactus and greenery led to the sturdy wooden hut. The timber covered bar was decorated in a nautical theme and fully stocked with liquor. Round nautical balls hung from the ceiling and lifebuoys lined the walls. A white Bahamian, or Conchy-Joe greeted us with a smile. "Welcome to Mac Duff's. Are you here for a few days?"

"Just one night," Nick answered.

"What a shame," he said. "Only one night in paradise. Well, I'm Kevin. If there's anything I can do for you."

"Restrooms," I mumbled.

"Out back," he pointed. "Outhouse style. One for the guys and one for the ladies."

I grinned. "How interesting."

A single thin slice of plywood divided the men's room from the ladies which housed only the necessities; a flushable toilet and toilet paper. When I returned Kevin was making four Goombay Smashes, a combination of spiced and coconut rum, grenadine and pineapple. He told us he owned the bar and adjacent cottage rentals. He offered to give us a tour of the property once we had our drinks in hand.

"What's the story with the duck?" I asked.

He looked at me. "It gets nervous if a portal to a third dimension is opened. It senses it."

My eyes widened as my companions laughed. Kevin chortled while handing me a drink. "Your friends here put me up to saying that." When his amusement subsided he continued. "Actually, the duck has been staring out to sea and pacing for a few months now." He glanced towards the beach, "A boat traveling through left it on shore, and then took off with her ducklings still on board. She's been looking and waiting for them ever since."

My heart sank as I reacted in unison with Jamie, "Awe."

"So she's waiting for her babies to return?" Jamie asked.

Kevin shrugged, "It appears so."

I glanced out to the beach at it, still pacing. How sad to have your babies disappear, and then to spend your entire life waiting for them to return when they never would. It followed a basic motherly instinct. Years ago as a senior in college, I had a miscarriage. The loss devastated my soul, and it took me months to recover my strength. The poor duck would never be happy again, or in any way normal if she kept awaiting their return. I overcame the despair, so perhaps she could do the same.

My sad thoughts were interrupted by Nick declaring "Let's go look at the cottages."

The five of us trotted next door clasping our drinks. It was a warm and cozy two bedroom with a kitchenette and a single bathroom. Bright pink on the outside, a lively combination of yellow, lime green and cobalt blue painted the interior. "Very cute," I commented. "But don't most people stay on their boat?"

"We have an airport in our back yard," Kevin chirped.

"Now we're talking," Lucas said, "Let's check it out."

Kevin pointed us in the direction of the airstrip, agreeing to meet us back at the bar for a refill. We found a short runway, only 3,300 feet long and filled with potholes, cracks and weeds.

"Wow, this would be challenging to fly into," I said.

"Well there's a fascinating history to this airport. It was once controlled by Pablo Escobar and his cohort Carlos Lehder back in the late 70's and early 80's." Nick said. "Lehder owned the island and used it to smuggle cocaine from Columbia to the United States. Armed guards patrolled in jeeps and helicopters." He stopped for a moment and motioned to the runway. "And this landing strip was only used for his drug trade. Other planes were forbidden or even worse, their occupants killed. Drugs and money flowed, women ran around naked, and people had sex everywhere."

I smirked and glanced at Jamie for her reaction.

"It's true." She said, "Nick studies his history."

"Have you ever seen the movie *Blow*, with Johnny Depp?" Nick asked.

I searched my mind for Johnny Depp drug movies set in the Bahamas and recalled a reporter trying to land in a small plane in the Bahamas only to be captured or turned away. "I think so."

"It's in part based on the drug trade here. Depp plays George Jung, a drug partner of Lehder. Both were part of the Medellin Cartel with Escobar as the head honcho." I listened intensely as we all strolled. "They murdered, kidnapped and bribed their way into using the island as the base of their smuggling operation. They were thugs who made billions. They're all dead or imprisoned now," he concluded.

"Wow. I'd like to excavate there. I'll have to re-watch the movie when we get back to the states."

"I have a book on the boat you can read called, *Turning the Tide*. Nick shook his near empty glass as the ice hit the plastic walls, "Shall we get a refill."

The three of them turned around and walked back to Mac Duff's, I lingered imagining the island bustling with small Cessna's, uniformed drug smugglers with AK47's, garbage bags full of cocaine, and naked women. I may have liked partying here on the island, with no rules for a week or so, but then the debauchery would have worn thin. I envisioned digging up bullets, degenerated bags of cocaine, skeletal remains of murder victims, and maybe even thousands of dollars of hidden drug money.

A flashback to one of my first archaeological digs in California came to mind. Brushing off human skulls and bones with a toothbrush for eight hours a day was intriguing, until I fell asleep at night and my dreams turned to nightmares. For weeks they penetrated my lurid nighttime reality, until one day they just stopped. The human souls staring back and tormenting me gave up and became peaceful again, freeing me to pursue my career.

I glanced ahead and caught up to the others at the end of the runway, steps away from the beach club. A group of four strangers sat at the bar chatting with Kevin. "Another round?" he asked, noticing our arrival.

"Sounds good," Jamie answered.

We ordered conch fritter appetizers with our drinks and struck up idle chat with the couples at the bar. They'd just arrived by sailboat and were staying for the week. Previously at the neighboring Highborne Cay and working their way down to Cat Island, they were enjoying a trip of a lifetime over the next few months. We were the only two boats anchored in the harbor, and the only visitors currently on the small island. Kevin seemed to enjoy the company, since he was one of the few permanent residents here.

What a lonely life, I thought. *To be so disconnected from the rest of the world with just a neurotic duck and a few helpers in the restaurant for company.* I guessed Kevin and his business depended on fleeting travelers arriving by boat mostly, or the occasional private plane. It's a lifestyle few could live.

Another round of drinks arrived, along with a small order of conch fritters. As the sun sank in the sky, we elected to return to *Cabin Fever* for dinner and a good night's rest.

Mosquitoes swarmed us as we left the beach club, dashed past the pacing bird, into the ocean and back aboard the Bluewater. Scurrying through the sliders, the four of us shut the critters out. "I need a quick shower," I announced as I headed for the bathroom to wash off the attack and the salt I'd accumulated. Five minutes later I emerged itch free. "Anyone else?" I asked. "It's soothing."

Jamie kept busy in the galley prepping burgers and Lucas scooted by with a quick, "I'm going to rinse off."

Nick called me over to the couch. He held a book in his hand as if it was the Bible, raising it high, then gracefully placing it in my willing hands. *"The Turning of the Tides, One Man Against the Medellin Cartel,"* he said with an uplifting smile. "It's based on a true story and will give you a more complete picture of the importance of this island during the cocaine wars of the 70's and 80's."

I placed it on my lap, "Thank you. I'll start reading it tonight or tomorrow." On the cover I noticed a downed plane in the shallow water surrounded by hammerhead sharks. "One Deadly Summer," it read above the title.

"I think you'll enjoy it now that you've seen the island," he beamed.

"Yes I will." I dashed off to lay the book on my bed, then went to help Jamie in the galley. I opened a bottle of Pinot Grigio, pouring a glass for each of us. "Nick, do you want wine with dinner?" I called out.

"No. Rum and coke, please." I mixed him one and then made a vodka and cranberry for my lover.

As I set the table Lucas appeared, declaring, "The toilets aren't working. I've tried flushing both. I think the vacuum system is broken."

Jamie looked up, "Oh, that's not good."

The guys went to troubleshoot the situation.

We piled the plates with burgers and salad. "This is the veggie burger," Jamie pointed to one, setting them on the table.

The boys returned frowning. Nick took his seat on the circular bench lining the table, followed by the rest of us. "So it looks like we have no working toilets until we get some parts," Nick said. "If you need to pee in the middle of the night, go ahead. Just no toilet paper." He squished his bun to the burger. "Anything else, either jump in the water or use the outhouse behind the restaurant."

I had an aversion to outhouses. While doing some archaeological work in Newport Beach, I'd often slip away with another female co-worker to use the bathrooms at a nearby Starbucks instead of the porta potties on-site. The small enclosure, combined with my fear of an earthquake was enough to make me cringe. My lips turned upward in a slight smile at the thought. I looked at my veggie burger without interest.

Picking at my food and changing the subject, I asked. "Do I have time to run tomorrow? What's the schedule?"

"We have none," Jamie sang. "We're in the Bahamas, mon."

Nick shot Jamie a dismissive glance. "Well, that's not entirely true. I'd say we should be on our way by noon. So a leisurely morning, followed by an early afternoon departure."

"Nice," I mumbled as I finally took a bite of my burger.

"You can run the runway," Lucas chimed in.

"I just might. It'll be interesting jumping into the water to reach land where I can run." I tilted my head. "I don't usually start my run wet, although I always end up soaked at the end."

"Or you can run back and forth with the duck," he said sarcastically.

Jamie laughed as I shot him a sideways look. His smirk widened as he finished his burger in one bite, "Just saying. Today is the fastest I've ever seen you swim."

I paused, taking a sip of wine. "Only because I had a two-hundred-pound bull shark on my tail named Lucas."

"Well, I want you to be comfortable in the water by the end of this trip." He took a sip from his glass without relaxing his gaze. "I'll teach you some different techniques."

***

I read the first few chapters of *Turning the Tide*, until my eyes grew heavy and I drifted into dreams of drug trafficking and artifact smuggling. My statue multiplied into thousands, stuffed with cocaine. They were loaded into Cessnas guarded and piloted by the Cartel soldiers wearing olive green military garb. The idols were identical, all mimicking Uga-Bugga with the drugs stuffed into the hole on its head. Then in midair a chute released thousands of drug-stuffed idols into the Gulf Stream off the coast of Fort Lauderdale where boats were waiting to collect the effigies bobbing in the water like floating corks. Several blue and white Intrepid boats similar to the one we were towing held my parents and grandparents and other faceless people collecting idols with nets. They were happy, almost giddy. Until a monster wave caused them to panic, and I woke from my dream.

CHAPTER SEVEN

MAY 29, 2011

EXUMAS

Wading through the water, I spotted the duck pacing, and wondered if it slept at night or if ducks dreamed, recalling my crazy vision of drug-stuffed idols. Heading towards the runway, I passed Kevin and waved with a quick flip of my right hand. Sea Grapes edged the landing strip as I caught a glimpse of the ocean in the distance.

With music blaring through my iPod, I barely heard the faint sound of an engine landing behind me. Suddenly, a Piper Aztec touched down next to me and I jumped into the Sea Grape bushes in astonishment. What the hell? I guess jogging on a runway with music blasting in my ears probably wasn't a good idea. Continuing past the dilapidated airport I observed another plane resting in the shallow water just feet from the shoreline. It looked almost identical to the one on the cover of *Turning the Tide*. I scooted closer to the water's edge, embracing the moment of historical relevance, and then continued my jog along the shoreline until my turnaround point, where I headed back to the ship. The pacing duck greeted me for the last time.

Aboard the *Cabin Fever*, the crew intensely perused charts and discussed cruising plans as I arrived drenched in sweat and salt water. "Wow, I had an exciting morning," I exhaled while approaching the threesome on the bridge. "An Aztec landed and I saw the plane from the cover of the book."

The three looked up. "So you had a good run?" Jamie asked.

I nodded. "Yes, awesome."

"Good. We are setting sail soon, so if you need anything on land, now is the time to get it. Or if you need to use the toilet."

"Oh, good idea." I turned around and dove back into the water more confident of my swimming abilities. Dripping wet I visited the outhouse and mumbled a quick goodbye to Kevin as I walked by. After a swift shower, I dressed in my bathing suit, ready to tackle the day.

Once in the cabin, Lucas shared our plans for the day as we lunched on fresh baked cheese croissants. We would cruise past several small islands, then Lucas and I would jump into the Intrepid for some fishing and meet up with the Bluewater at Compass Cay. Then we'd make our way together toward Staniel Cay where we would retrieve the parts being flown in to fix the toilets. The ocean was flat calm and fairly shallow except for the Exuma Sound which dropped to almost 6000 feet, similar to the Tongue of the Ocean. We would fish these deep waters for dolphinfish, tuna, or anything we could catch for dinner or recreation. Sport fish like marlin and sailfish we'd catch and release, caught purely for the thrill of the fight. Anything we brought into the boat and gaffed was for consumption, not to be needlessly wasted.

I grabbed my book, cigarettes, a towel and a bottle of water, setting myself up for a few hours of sunbathing. "Anybody want to work on their tan?" I offered, organizing my belongings a large cushion at the stern.

"I'll join you," Jamie answered.

Returning minutes later she sat down on a cushion next to me, spraying tanning lotion on her shoulders, neck and face. Holding up her sun kissed brown bottle, "Would you like some?"

"Sure." I took the lotion from her outreached hand and sprayed my chest, my face already covered in SPF, a daily routine. I'd spent some time with Jamie, but I didn't really know her outside of the four of us having dinner a few times in Florida. I considered her a strong person, and I'd witnessed her command a room. She was a leader, while I only led when nobody else stepped up to the plate. Laying horizontal, I glanced sideways through my sunglasses. "So how did you and Nick meet?" I asked.

Her face lit up and an uncontrollable smile swept across her face. "Well, it's kind of a funny story." She glimpsed at me then skyward. "Have you heard about Columbus Day Regatta?"

I considered the question, answering, "Lucas said it's a party on the water, and he wants us to go this fall. September, right?"

"Yes, the first weekend in September, and party is an understatement. Everyone is drinking crazy amounts of alcohol, and bathing suits are optional. It's like an orgy in the middle of the ocean."

I cracked a smile. Jamie didn't seem like the orgy type. I didn't consider myself the type either, although I had an experimental incident or two in college. Another couple, another girl for the sake of being open-minded and trying it once without judgment. The experiences were enjoyable, but not mind-blowing or life-changing.

"So I took my boat down with about six girlfriends. At the time I had a thirty-six-foot Contender and we anchored next to Nick's fifty-four-foot Bertram. He had about ten guys on the boat and they started throwing beads at us to remove our tops. So I tossed my bikini, dove in the water and emerged on his stern." She propped herself up on her elbows and motioned to her breasts. "And he kept staring at these, so I said, are you going to get me a drink? Still stunned he handed me the one in his hand."

I giggled. "I'm sure he did."

Her thin smile widened. "We just really hit it off. It was a crazy weekend. All of my crew ended up spending the weekend on the Bertram. Naked guys and girls floated through the water party, gliding from boat to boat, music blared, and come Monday we decided to keep in touch. The Bertram and his captain stayed in Miami. Nick flew in from Texas almost every weekend." Her eyes sparkled, "That was almost eleven years ago."

"Do you go to the regatta every year?"

"No, but I'd like to go again this year." She laid back down, "It's fun, but a bit much at times."

"It sounds exciting. I'd like to check it out at least once. Where do people sleep, if you come on a smaller boat, like our Intrepid?" I caught myself referring to Lucas' boat as ours.

She laughed. "Wherever they fall. Most people are so wasted

they just pass out on the boat or don't sleep at all, or all sleep together," She chuckled.

"Interesting," I snickered. I felt my skin starting to burn, so I turned, belly flat against the cushion.

Cracking open my book, I began to read. Lucas approached, "Can I get you ladies anything?"

"No, I'm fine. Actually, can you put some sunscreen on my tattoo?"

"I'd love to, honey." He squirted the white liquid on his fingertips, gently rubbing it onto my upper left shoulder.

Jamie asked in a slightly southern twang, "So what's the wild hair figure playing a flute represent?"

"It's a Kokopelli, Native American like Raven." Lucas said before disappearing.

She gave me a blank look, so I clarified. "It's a Native American symbol relating to childbirth, agriculture, and music. He's also sort of a trickster." I propped myself up on both elbows. "It's an ancient Anasazi symbol. Today it's more closely related to the Hopi Pueblo tribes in Arizona. To me it represents replenishment and the playful side of me, which is why I got it tattooed on my upper left back. Kinda like my little fun angel." I neglected to say anything about my miscarriage, another deeper more personal meaning for the symbol.

"Oh how…"

She was interrupted by a shout from Nick. "Pirates ahead!"

Jamie jumped up, dashing toward the helm as I followed. "11:00 O'clock," He handed the binoculars to Lucas. "What do you see?"

He studied the water through the Bushnell's. "Six guys dressed in all black on an Intrepid."

"It's best to stay clear of them. I have a shotgun, but I'm sure they're better armed."

After looking through the binoculars a few fleeting times Lucas handed them back to Nick announcing, "They've switched course, and they're heading our direction. I think I should get on the Intrepid and protect the Bluewater, or outrun them. Two moving boats are better than one slow one with a $60,000 toy tied to it. They won't steal a slow boat."

Nick turned. "Good thinking. Do you have anything for protection, if needed?"

"A flare or two."

Lucas dove off the stern, swimming rapidly to the smaller boat. "Raves untie the line," Lucas yelled. Scurrying to help, I released the knot and threw the line onto the Intrepid's bow.

"Do you want me to go with you?" I asked loudly.

"No Raven, get to the helm," Nick called. For a moment Lucas paralleled our course, then took off in the opposite direction.

Where in the hell is he going? What about the protection he spoke of having with two boats? Now I could clearly see the men aboard the other Intrepid, the pirate ship. They were completely covered from head to toe in black, as if they wouldn't stand out. Black headbands, skin, shirts and jeans in this heat had to be unbearable. The boat looked almost identical to ours, but with three engines instead of two. My legs felt restless as I constantly shifted my stance. The pirates were heading straight towards us. I felt like we were a floating target, unable to escape an inevitable attack.

"Where in the hell did he disappear to?" Nick said, looking around wildly.

I rapidly scanned the horizon, faintly spotting our boat far to the rear. "I see him in the distance." I pointed behind us. "Can we call him on the VHF?"

Picking up the radio microphone he tensely answered, "Yes. But the pirates are probably listening, scanning the airwaves."

He tuned into channel 69, and pushed the side button while speaking into the plastic mouthpiece. "*Breakfast in Bimini*, come back."

"This is Lucas," came a crackle from the radio. "I'm just checking on the rest of our fleet."

Nick stood mouth ajar. "Stay within sight. They're heading towards us."

Clearly within view, it looked as if Ninjas had invaded the Caribbean. I knew we didn't have a fleet. Except for the sailboat at Normans, we hadn't seen another boat for days. Maybe the lie was a scare tactic employed by Lucas to thwart the pirates? I looked back, spotting our boat heading back towards us. The pirates were a few hundred feet off our bow and Lucas arrived just off our starboard side.

Nick grabbed his shotgun from the compartment under the controls, holding it by his side. A whizzing sound echoed above the water, followed by another hiss through the air. I inhaled sulfur.

Jamie scanned the horizon, focusing the telescopic tubes on the pirates. "Their boat is smoking. I think a flare landed on it." Jamie called out, handing the binoculars to Nick.

"Holy shit, the cabin is on fire." A slight smile crossed his face. "Lucas is a hell of a sharpshooter, he hit something flammable in the cabin. Maybe a cushion, clothes or drugs." He adjusted the focus while gazing through the lens. "I can't tell what he hit, but it's burning and spreading fast."

Nick shifted our course east, away from the crippled pirate boat. I picked up the Bushnell's and glancing past him I saw the men scurrying around the cockpit trying to extinguish the fire. They were frantically dipping cups into the sea, throwing salt water onto the flames. Black smoke billowed from the door leading to the inside cabin. It radiated yellow and red, but it seemed contained. One man searched around the stern, looking for a bucket or fire extinguisher I imagined. I spotted a large gun on the floor, next to the helm.

"Where's Lucas?" I asked, anxiously looking in all directions.

"Ahead of us on the port side." Nick said. He increased speed, shifting his gaze from the bow to the motionless smoldering boat. After a few minutes he picked up the VHF microphone, "Good job Lucas. Slow down a bit and I'll follow you until we're out of sight."

From behind, Jamie swung her arms around Nick's waist as he navigated. "Good job captain."

She inched towards me for a one-armed hug around the neck. I welcomed the love and sensation of victory, although I still felt like we were in danger. The gun I spotted looked ten times more menacing than Nick's shotgun. I glanced over at the stationary pirate boat, now smaller on the horizon.

"I saw a gun on the deck," I said.

"I saw it too Raves. But they'll be busy with the fire for a while." Nick said. "And I only saw one. They may have more in the cabin." He paused, looking back at the ship. "If so, the bullets could explode inside the guns disabling them."

"Have you encountered pirates at sea before?" I asked.

"Noooo," Jamie whispered loudly.

"You hear about these things and prepare for them, but they're not common." Nick glanced back at me. "They are opportunists, meaning they don't want to run huge risk factors to get their booty.

We showed we can be a problem for them, and we will put up a fight." He cleared his throat. "And we had another, faster boat watching us. Lucas put himself in danger, but he's a hell of a marksman," he said.

The realization he could have been in real trouble alone alarmed me, and I looked back to make sure he was close. He slowly approached on the port side. I scanned the water for the pirates, now just a minuscule speck in the otherwise lonely sea. Our direction shifted south, back on track towards Compass Cay.

"Raves, I really need a beer. Can you throw me one?" Lucas called from *Breakfast in Bimini.*

Seizing a cold bottle from the small fridge I scurried down the stairs, reaching over the side rail and handing it to him. Sweat covered his face, beads forming near his sandy blonde hairline, continually rolling down to his thick eyebrows and the sides of his face. "Are you going to tie up to *Cabin Fever*?

"No, I think it's best if I just run alongside. You can hop in and we'll fish for a bit." He twisted the cap off his beer, taking a swig. "I need to calm my nerves."

"I'm sure. I hope they don't come back."

He took another swig, "I don't think they will. I'm going to cruise around here within Nick's sight and check things out. If you could pack the small cooler with some beers, I'll be back to get you." He pulled and lit a cigarette from the radio box where he always kept a stash. "And another pack of cigarettes, please."

I spontaneously air blew a kiss by pressing and pouting my lips together, a slight squeak escaping my mouth. "Okay Captain."

I packed about eight beers from the inside refrigerator, and covered them in ice, placing a pack of cigarettes in a side pocket and set the bag near the slider. I shared our intentions with the Kramers, who thought it was a great idea and then returned to my sunbathing spot. Reading my book, I occasionally glanced up as we passed several small cays. The translucent opal water hitting their shores was breathtaking. The serene panorama freed my mind from the possibility of another pirate encounter. I wondered if they extinguished the fire or if it consumed the boat.

"Honey," I heard Lucas's voice.

"See you in a bit," I enthusiastically called out to the helm as I ran down to meet my lover. I grabbed the cooler, hanging it over the railing for Lucas to catch in a short drop. "Okay, how do I get aboard?"

"You have to jump in the water, and swim to the ladder."

"Seriously?" My stomach turned as uncontrolled nervousness overtook my body.

I have to get used to this, I told myself as I scanned the water for sharks. I jumped overboard, calmed my initial panic and paddled underwater until I reached the ladder. The ocean felt amazing, like diving into a pool of slightly chilled champagne, buoyant and bubbly against my body. I emerged with a refreshed smile. "This is definitely paradise," I said softly.

"If we take away the pirates."

And my anxiety and fear around water.

"Yes it is," he glowed. He waved to the Kramers as we pulled away to a slow troll towards the Exuma Sound. "I'm going to put a few lines out. Can you steer?"

I took the controls like an old pro as he went about prepping the fishing rods and letting them out to a distance he deemed reasonable. He focused on the task at hand, like a blue heron hunting for fish at sunrise. I could almost see the gears turning in his head. He looked at all the different colored lures in different sizes, choosing just the right one for each of the four rods. He selected a red and silver speckled lure, a yellow and blue one, a plain silver slightly larger lure and another silver one blended with crimson. Each had a purpose, and the distance seemed equally planned. Satisfied with his rigging and spacing behind the boat, he secured all rods in holders. Lucas took back the cockpit controls.

I gave him a look of admiration he must have sensed. After a long silence he finally said, "What?"

I tilted my head, holding my gaze. "I noticed your passion for fishing. How did you learn?"

"As far back as I can remember, I've been fishing. When I was eight or so my dad taught me a few things." He increased the speed slightly. "We rented a boat and fished on the Potomac, when he had time. I really enjoyed the moments we spent together on the water, so I learned how to fish to make him proud. Sometimes I'd ride my bike to the river bank. Although I threw most of the fish back, I found it very peaceful and a thrill every time I got a bite." He shifted course slightly right. "Can you grab me a beer?"

"Yes." I fetched two from the cooler and returned to his side.

"So by the time we moved to Florida from Virginia, I associated fishing with enthusiasm." He paused and took a swig from his beer. "I'd fish on the canal behind our house almost every day after school. Then my dad bought me a small boat, and I trolled up and down the canal, eventually venturing into the ocean. Most of the time, it was catch and release, which helped me gain a respect for the fish I set free."

A toasty smile lit up his face, making me smile. "Now the ocean's a different story. I'd read all the fishing magazines on what type of lures or bait to use so I'd go out on my own and try different things. One day while bouncing around in three to four foot seas not too far offshore, the line started whizzing like crazy." His voiced intensified as he imitated reeling. "So I grabbed it and reeled and reeled and it seemed to get nowhere. I really fought this fish hard. Well, I pulled in a fifty pound dolphinfish," he said, spreading his hands wide to show me its size.

"Wow that's big," I agreed.

"It's huge for a thirteen-year-old catching his first fish in the Atlantic. Anyway, I was hooked after that for sure."

"Too bad you couldn't share it with your dad," I solemnly whispered, realizing his desire to please a workaholic father.

He remained silent, so I prodded some more. "I bet you didn't release that one."

"Nope, I took it home for my step-mom to cook."

"Was she a good cook?"

"Yes, but she made me clean it. So I learned how to skin and filet." He chuckled. "It was my first attempt and a bit crude. And then she taught me how to fry it."

I smiled. "I'm glad one of us can cook, because I'm not so inclined. I can reheat, and microwave."

"Not true. You made me a killer eggplant parmesan when we first started dating."

"I'm glad you liked it honey." I didn't tell him I just stacked frozen pre-breaded cutlets, poured marinara on it and smothered it in cheese. I wanted him to think I had some domestic tendencies. And some day when I had time, I'd learn how to cook.

I glimpsed over at the larger boat in the distance cruising at a steady pace. Behind us the fishing lines were barely noticeable and the reels quiet. "Did Nick or Jamie ever tell you how they met? She shared their first encounter at the Columbus Day Regatta."

He smirked, "Yes, I was there. On the Bertram with Nick and a bunch of other guys."

"Oh, I didn't realize you knew Nick so long," I took a sip of beer. "I'd like to check out the Regatta this year."

"I sold Nick his Bertram, and we've been buddies ever since. And I'd love to take you this fall. I think you'll..."

The lines screeched and screamed as Lucas yelled, "Grab the rod and start reeling."

I ran to the spinning reel and started turning the knob in the aluminum rod holder as fast as I could manage. Lucas slapped a white plastic belt around my waist and placed the rod in the socket now resting on my stomach.

"Keep reeling. Give it some up and down movement. Put your entire body into it like this." He bent forward a bit, then back as he imitated spinning the rod in his right hand. Then he disappeared to the helm. "Stay with it."

"I'm trying."

I danced forward and backward, constantly spinning my arm like a wheel in motion. I wasn't sure who would tire first, me or the fish. I felt more resistance then a bit of slack as I searched the water for my monster fish to appear. Moving right and left slightly and up and down constantly, my arm started to feel like a lead pipe. "My arm hurts," I called out.

"Stay with it." He encouraged. "This is your fish." He lit a cigarette, with his eyes constantly darting right and left. "Don't lose it."

I kept up the fight as the boat slowly trolled at a snail's pace. Nick's voice came through the radio, "What did you hook?"

"We don't know yet," Lucas shot back.

"I see something silver near the boat," I hollered.

He appeared next to me peering into the sea with a gaff in his hand.

"Do we have to gaff it?" I pleaded.

"No. I think you can bring this one up. It's small enough."

Persevering with my reeling, Lucas reached the end of the line unhooking the fish as it floundered around the fiberglass base of the stern. "It's a blackfin tuna," he declared. "And it's legal."

I clapped lightly. "It's not a bad size."

He picked up the tuna and placed it in the cooler. "Good job honey."

"We have sushi," Lucas called into the VHF.

"There's a nice deserted island ahead of us if you guys want to stop there and splash in the water," Nick said.

"Sounds good. See you there."

We trolled another half hour without a bite. Lucas asked me to 'bring the lines in' and I felt like a pro after catching the first fish of my life. I'd seen others do it, but I never took the rod myself. Now I saw the rush involved, especially catching. I looked forward to sampling my catch with some soy and wasabi.

Cabin Fever lowered her anchor just feet from the small island. We ran full throttle onto the powdery shoreline. I braced for impact. I heard a small thud and saw a big grin from my lover. "We're here."

"Why did we park on the beach?"

"The tide's going out. It's safe here."

I shrugged. "Okay."

Lucas climbed down the ladder perched in the shallow aquamarine surf. "Can you hand me the tuna? I'm going to swim it over to the big boat. Pick it up by its tail."

I reluctantly hoisted the slimy creature by its tail gingerly passing it to Lucas at arm's length. "Yuck," I mumbled. "I'm glad I don't have to filet it. I really don't like anything dead or bloody."

He rolled his eyes. "You'd easily perish out here. Good thing you have me to provide for us. Didn't you inherit hunting, fishing and gathering from your Native American ancestors?"

"I have the gathering part down, and the eating, and drinking. I'm coming in, do you need anything?"

"A beer and a cigarette."

"I'll bring them." I pulled two beers from the cooler and lit two cigarettes then did a balancing act down the ladder. The water reached my waist and felt just as refreshing as earlier in the day. Reaching Lucas, I handed him one of each, simultaneously grinning at Jamie hanging over the rail struggling to grab the tuna.

"Your first fish," she said, holding it up by its tail. "I'll have Nick clean it."

I danced and swayed in the water, floated on my back, and enjoyed my two vices, smoking and drinking. My skin radiated a sun-kissed glow from the past few days of sunbathing. I used sunscreen ritually, but my skin bronzed easily to a dark tan, a look I welcomed. It contrasted with my now sundrenched chestnut hair reflecting reddish blonde highlights, white bathing suit, and the serene natural beauty surrounding us.

"We have Sashimi," Jamie purred over the rail.

I climbed up the Bluewater, a bit hungry for an afternoon snack and eager to taste my first catch. Lucas followed. The anticipation was akin to a child baking her first batch of cookies. I remembered baking with my friends for the first time without the help of adults. With youthful rawness, we had forgotten one major ingredient, flour. The cookies turned out to be a chocolate buttery joy, as we giggled and devoured our creations. The memorable bonding of six tween girls one unforgettable summer at our beach house. I didn't clean or prep this tuna, but I was still proud and giddy.

"Beautiful presentation," I complimented Jamie while entering the cabin. "Thanks for preparing it. I want to learn."

"I'll teach you during the trip if you're interested."

Not sure if I could get past cleaning bloody dead things, I answered, "I'm always open to learning new things."

The Sashimi melted in my mouth with sensations of salty soy, intense sinus clearing wasabi and soft fresh tuna teasing my senses. "Um, so good," I whispered. It tasted better than any store bought or restaurant served sushi I'd had. It was not only my first catch, but my first truly fresh off the boat raw experience. The rest of the crew took a few pieces seemingly unmoved, while I was nearly orgasmic.

After a few more bites, Jamie proposed checking out the island with tumblers full of rum punch since she'd made some while we were out fishing. I filled the glasses, passing them out over the railing as we found our way back into the sea and to shore.

Wandering around the deserted cay, I sought out shells and sea glass, making a nice pile on the beach. Lucas floated in the water, as the Kramers leisurely walked the shore holding hands. Not a single structure existed on the island, or any sign of human life. Noticing my honey walking towards and studying the Intrepid, I picked up my pile and turned his direction. He paced around it frowning.

I dropped my shell stash in the sand at the bow of *Breakfast in Bimini*. "What's wrong, sweets?"

"Look at the boat," he mused.

"It's completely out of water. I didn't think the tide would get this low."

My eyes widened as I realized our predicament. "What do we

need to do?"

"Well the good news is the tide is coming back in," he sighed. "The bad news is it needs to come in faster. We need to get to Compass tonight and we are at the mercy of the ocean."

"Can we pull it out with the big boat?"

"No. Can't risk hitting ground with both." He paused, gears turning in his head. "We can loosen the sand around it and try and push it closer to the water." Leaving his drink on the ground, he squatted under the port side near the bow and began pawing ditches. I followed his lead, kneeling and shoveling sand away from the hull. I felt like a kitten in a giant litter box, neurotically digging seemingly endless amounts of pale powder.

"Now let's go to the other side," he said, winded. We repeated the motions on the starboard edge, quickly excavating with fingers and hands.

I felt the Kramer's approach with faint footsteps, the light obscured by a partial shadow. "This isn't good," Nick rumbled.

Lucas and I stood simultaneously. "Well the tide's coming back in and I think if we could clear some sand and push it back..."

"Hold on. Did you say push it back?" Nick flabbergasted. "This isn't a dingy."

"The tide's coming in, and it's reached the stern. If we could just loosen the sand to make it easier for the water to surround the boat, then we can try to push it. I don't know what else to do." Lucas seemed frustrated.

Nick hesitated. "I'll get the starboard and you get the port. Ladies, watch the boat and if there's any leaning let me know. This isn't the smartest thing to do."

The guys bent under the hull, digging the sand away as if they were building a moat around a large sandcastle. Jamie and I looked at each other and the boat from every angle. The tide rose in barely noticeable increments. The men emerged, covered in sweat as we all stood back, staring at the boat and tide. I realized intently watching the tide was like trying to watch your toenails grow.

"Okay, Nick let's try to push from the bow."

Jamie and I stood back as the guys made an attempt. The boat didn't budge. They tried a second time, still nothing.

"Damn," Lucas blurted out. "I guess it's onto plan B." I hoped the backup plan is better than the current tone.

I was about to ask when Jamie chirped, "What's plan B?"

"Compass Cay is only 25 nautical miles from here. For the Intrepid, it's less than an hour but over two and a half on the Bluewater." He turned towards Nick, "Raves and I will wait for the tide and you guys head towards Compass."

"Considering the sun is setting in two hours it's a good idea," Nick consented. "We have a small area of concern with some coral heads, but it's not an issue in the daytime. He raised his eyebrows at Lucas. "Are you okay with this? You know where you're going?" He asked with a bit of uncertainty.

"Yes, once the boat's back in the water, I'll go full speed ahead." He grinned. "I just ask for one thing."

"What's that?"

"The pitcher of rum punch."

Nick snorted, "Priorities."

"Um, so the pirates are no longer a threat?" I asked.

The three glared at me and Nick responded. "It's always a possibility, but the likelihood of twice in one day is well...slim. The bigger risk is getting stuck out here after sunset."

I rocked my hips side to side. "Just saying, luck hasn't really been on our side the past few days.

He shot me a sideways look, dismissing my remark. "See you in Compass Raves."

"Bon Voyage."

I stood at the shoreline while Lucas followed the Kramers, returning with a full pitcher of rum punch. Sitting on the shore while sipping our drinks, we watched them depart. I felt like waving as if the Love Boat set sail. I hummed the Love Boat theme.

"Are you humming the Love Boat?"

"Yes." I grinned, "So is this your idea of getting me alone on a deserted island?"

His eyes sparkled, a mischievous smile lighting up his face. "Since you mention it..."

He leaned in towards me as I took off into the ocean. "You have to catch me," I provocatively challenged.

"Is that a dare?"

"Yup." I bobbed up and down in the ocean, my groin stirring with anticipation.

"I can see your titty hard-on from here," he called out, walking towards me.

"T H O," I teased, removing and throwing my bathing suit top onto the beach, immediately bobbing back into the ocean.

His steadfast pace and stare excited me. I slowly hopped back against the incoming waves, dancing leg to leg, grinning ear to ear. I could feel my wetness and desire, an uncontrolled natural response. My sensual floodgates opened along with an innate carnal yearning. My bikini bottoms were soaked from the inside out. He approached underwater like a shark sizing up its prey, emerging directly in front of me.

"What are you going to do? I won't go willingly," I provoked, hoping he would take the dominant lead.

"Oh really." He grabbed my ass cheeks with his large firm hands, lifting me onto his hips. My legs naturally wrapped around his waist as he spun us 180 degrees, steadily drifting towards the beach. "You don't need to be willing, I'm stronger, and you have nowhere to go."

So true, I thought. *He could do anything, and I couldn't do much about it.* No place to run, nobody to call for help, absolutely defenseless, I felt safe with him. It turned me on, my sanctuary amidst the lust.

He gently placed me on the beach while passionately kissing my salty lips. Gliding down my body he tenderly licked my breasts, his long-lashed green eyes watching my reaction. My tongue traced my lips and the corner of my mouth as uninhibited groans escaped me. His hands lightly traveled along on the side of my waist, his kisses tracing a path to my stomach. He outlined circles around my turquoise bead piercing, dodging a moist tongue in and out of my navel. My back naturally arched, hips shifting upwards toward him, my yearning growing stronger, almost unbearable. I groaned and reached down for his hard-on.

"Not yet," he admonished.

He paused, removed my bikini bottoms, continuing down my fuzzy auburn happy trail to my inner thigh. Lingering around my vagina for a moment with his warm breath, he finally teased my clit with his tongue. I groaned. He vibrated my clit slowly, and then rapidly, responding to my unspoken need. I called out, "Fuck, I'm going to come already." He looked up with wanting eyes. I closed mine as I felt the sensation of the sun hitting my skin, his moist tongue on my sensitive clit, and soft sounds of waves hitting the beach. I raised my pelvis towards his mouth and whispered, "Don't stop. It feels so good." Followed by a whimper and shake. He stopped for a few seconds recognizing my orgasm, and then continued to lick, as if finishing an ice cream cone. "Fuck," I screamed. "I'm going to come again." I shook and groaned some more, before completely letting go, "Wow."

"Turn over," he breathed. "Doggie-style." I flipped over, desperately wanting him inside me. "You're soaked," he whispered.

"Yes, that's what you do to me."

He entered me like a rocket as we moved with perfect symmetry. I could feel him getting harder, nearing orgasm. "Come on my ass," I breathed. He let out an uncontrollable grunt, squirting liquid on my lower back, ass and thigh. We melted, laying side by side in the sand.

"Wow. Amazing, and a first." I sighed looking at the horizon as I rested my head on his chest. "My first time having sex on the beach on a deserted island."

He exhaled, "Yes it was."

We rested as the waves splashed our feet. I glanced back at the boat, nudging Lucas. "The water's filling the moat."

"Do you mean the boat?"

"No, the ditch surrounding the boat. The moat."

He glanced back. "We're getting there." He stood to examine the progress, "A little bit longer until full high tide." He glanced at our half empty glasses and the pitcher. "Would you like a post sex cocktail?"

"I'd love one," I beamed. "Then we can walk the island naked."

He lingered near the Intrepid, accessing the situation.

I leisurely strolled the beach realizing how much I cherished Lucas. I'd only known him for six months, and we'd been intimate for a little over four. I'd had boyfriends over the years, a few casual relationships, but nothing meaningful since college. I focused most of my energy on work, both as a museum director and archaeologist. My social life also revolved around the museum, friends and colleagues getting together for dinner, movies and games. I'd play *Dungeons and Dragons* with my coworkers so I didn't have to spend the weekend with just my cat, Karma. Meeting Lucas changed everything. Now, here I was in the middle of nowhere walking naked on a deserted island. We had killer sex and watched the most beautiful sunset into the azure water with a rum punch in my hand. Nothing could be better, and I felt on top of the world.

As I returned with another handful of sun-bleached shells, he called out from the helm, "We're good to go."

I put my bikini back on and climbed aboard *Breakfast in Bimini*. The sun disappeared as we advanced the throttle. He seemed a bit nervous crossing so late across an area of known coral heads, and gave the darkening water his undivided attention.

Behind us I spotted a similar boat speeding our direction. "Honey, I think the pirates are behind us. It looks like the same boat and it's fast."

Without looking he pushed full throttle as we stood side by side, bouncing across the sea surface.

CHAPTER EIGHT

MAY 30, 2011

COMPASS AND STANIEL CAY

"Get out," I heard a raspy whisper. My eyes instantly opened. "What?" I whispered back into the air, glancing over at Lucas peacefully sleeping. I looked past him to a sliver of light peeking through the small window. "Ugh," I muttered, quietly climbing out of bed.

Giving the idol on the floor the evil eye, I put on my running clothes, skipping coffee and the sometimes distracting music on my iPod.

I stumbled onto the dock, scanning Compass Cay for any activity. Only four boats were docked at the marina. On the stern of a rather large vessel sat a lady in a swimsuit sipping from a mug. Noticing her turn my direction, I waved. We seemed to be the only ones awake at the crack of dawn.

Finding a trail along the marina, I began my trot. Without my iPod, thoughts of my strange dreams and the idol engulfed me. Is it all an illusion and just my overactive imagination?

Am I just having strange dreams like the ones I've been prone to all my life? After all, I'd had nightmares and bizarre dreams when I was a child and as an adult I rarely recall them. When I did, they were otherworldly. The normalcy of an earthly life is unknown in my memorable visions. I recalled one where the earth was spinning off its axis and microwaves wouldn't work. Somehow, everyone craved popcorn, but couldn't microwave the hard kernels. In my sleep, I felt the heaviness of gravity, and it shocked me into consciousness. The malicious voice this daybreak seemed genuine, external, and nothing my mind could subconsciously invent. Was the source the statue I had found? I had to find the origin and meaning of the mysterious idol.

As I approached a crossroad, my mind shifted from the ethereal to the natural beauty humbly presenting itself. I stopped in awe. The flat rugged scrub trail gave way to a translucent opal lagoon. Aquamarine, jade and lazuli waters splashed against the pure porcelain colored sand. Seagulls yapped, "Cacaw, Cacaw". Palm tree fronds brushed against each other in the wind, sounding like a rake scrapping leaves in the fall. Continuing my run along the trail I paralleled the bejeweled cove, water lapping against the deserted shore.

I arrived back at the marina drenched in sweat. "Good morning sweetie," I called out to Lucas when I saw him sipping coffee on the dock. "Did you sleep in?" I teased, considering I was usually the last one out of bed.

He smirked. "What got your butt out of bed so early?"

"Ugh," I sighed. "I had another weird dream. Something whispered for me to get out of bed."

He spit his coffee with a spray and a chuckle. "I whisper that to you all the time, but you ignore me."

"Well you don't have a creepy voice," I shot back. "And it said, get out. Like a warning." I squinted at him through my sunglasses. "I think the idol is telling me something and it's cursed."

"Honey, your imagination is just out of control sometimes." He took a long sip from his mug, dismissing the gloomy voice. "Nick and I are taking the Intrepid to Staniel, to get the parts we need for the toilet. The plane is landing soon. It should be an easy fix once we get back, then we'll snorkel the cave this afternoon."

"Cave?"

"Yes. It's pretty fun." He took a final swig, spotting Nick approaching the dock he handed me his mug.

"You ready?" Nick asked Lucas, quickly darting his eyes toward me. "Good morning, Raven."

"Morning," I mumbled back, scooting past them. "Our slim chance of seeing the pirates again happened."

"And you're here safely." He turned to Lucas, "So you really just went full throttle without looking back?"

"Of course, what else could I do?" Lucas said. "If I hesitated, it could've gotten us into a really bad situation. Raves saw the boat, and I knew I wasn't taking any chances."

"It looked like the same boat. It sped towards us, but they didn't gain much momentum. At one point it appeared closer, but I couldn't make out how many people were onboard or what they were wearing. Once I saw Compass in the distance they disappeared."

***

"We'll have a working toilet, soon." Jamie sang from the galley when I returned from the marina showers.

"The marina facilities are pretty nice," I said. "And there are a handful of nurse sharks hanging out under the dock." I pointed in the direction of the sharks and then in the direction of the trailhead. "The trail is beautiful and takes you to a lagoon, one of the most stunning views I've seen."

"Sounds like you've been exploring." She wore a blue and white striped bathing suit with a towel thrown over her shoulder and water bottle in hand. "Will you be joining me on the bridge for sunbathing?"

"I'd love to. I'll see you up there." I changed into my purple paisley suit, tied my hair into a ponytail and quickly downed a lukewarm croissant. I eyed the beers, looked at the clock and opted for a water bottle.

The faint sound of jazz hummed from the neighboring boat. Relaxing, calm notes permeated the air as the perfect accoutrement to a fresh, briny breeze. I sat on the lounge chair next to Jamie.

"So, you were up early." She glanced up from her Martha Stewart magazine.

I must have the reputation as a slacker. I used to get up early all the time, but I'd been a bit more relaxed since I moved to Florida. "Another strange dream awoke me at dawn," I answered.

"What kind of dream?" Jamie directed her attention to me, placing her opened magazine next to her.

"A voice said, get out." I turned toward her, propping up on my left forearm. "A creepy, demanding voice. I couldn't get back to sleep, so I went for a beautiful early morning run."

I could see her eyes narrow through her sunglasses. "Are you prone to bad dreams?"

I paused. "Well, they come in and out of my life." I shifted in the recliner more towards the sky, a bit uncomfortable with oversharing. "Mostly, when I was younger, not so much in my adult years. When I started drinking, the bad dreams went away."

She snickered. "So you silenced the nightmares with alcohol? A bit of self-medication?"

I shrugged and chuckled. "As a teenager I'd overanalyze them. My mom took me to see a shrink, but nothing helped."

Her eyes narrowed even more and I felt her gaze intensify. "Raves, were you abused as a child?"

"Oh, God no. I had the most protective mother in the world." I paused, picking up a lighter off the deck floor, unconsciously twirling it between my fingers. "I have gaps in my childhood memories, but nothing leads me to believe I was abused."

"Any uncomfortable memories, or are most of them pleasant?" She asked.

"Most are pretty generic. I do recall almost drowning in the Pacific Ocean when I was very young, maybe around eight. I rolled around in the surf and then I was pulled under, unable to escape. I ran out of air. I felt trapped and powerless. I tried to fight the rip-current, but I couldn't. The memory stops when I surrendered to the struggle. I must have been rescued, although I don't know how. I don't even know if it's real, or I imagined it. Sometimes with me the difference between dreams and reality is not always clear-cut. So I try not to get attached to them. But I still experience fear when I think about my near drowning."

Her gaze and smile warmed, her thin lips and eyes turning slightly upwards. "But your mom should know if it happened, right? Have you asked her if this memory is real?"

"I have. And she said it isn't, and it's my imagination."

"What about your father? Could you have been with him at the beach?"

I tilted my head with an unrelenting smirk, continuing to flip the lighter. "I don't know who my biological father is, other than he's Hopi and lives on a reservation, so I wouldn't have been with him. I'd go to the beach a few times a year with my mom for a short vacation from Vegas. She knew my step-father then, although they weren't married yet, just friends." I paused in reflection, "He is just as protective. An old hippie with an organic, vegetarian lifestyle. He owns an organic co-op store in San Pedro. If something happened on his watch, he would have shared it with my mother."

"I just find it hard to believe you have such a vivid memory yet nobody can confirm you almost drowned." She said. "That uncertainty would bother me."

"I dismissed my childhood drowning memory already, since I'll probably never know the truth." I shrugged. "I don't think my dreams, or nightmares have anything to do with my upbringing. They just come and go, but the past few days are different. I've had a few since I found the idol." I placed the lighter next to the lounger, picking up my water bottle and taking a sip. "Like they're some sort of message, even though I don't believe in the supernatural."

A thin, tight smile crossed Jamie's face. "The mind is a tricky thing. I've been fortunate never to have bad dreams." She loosened up a bit, placing her magazine back on her lap. "Just don't let it get to you. I'm a good listener, but you may benefit from a professional who can help you explore your memories in more detail."

I knew a shrink couldn't help me, but I answered, "Yes, thanks for listening. You're lucky not to be burdened with nightmares." I laid down, shifting my attention to the book Nick gave me, *Turning of the Tide*.

After reading several chapters, I began mulling over Jamie's last statement. Was my unconscious brain concocting voices? Were my nightmares internal or external?

I turned toward her. "So what do you mean by the mind being tricky?"

She glanced up from her magazine with raised eyebrows. "I just mean the mind is a powerful thing and sometimes what you focus on becomes your reality." She grinned, "And, we are in the Bermuda Triangle."

"You're very sage-like," I mumbled.

Pointing to the Intrepid pulling into the harbor, she hummed, "The boys are back."

With the parts they needed, it only took a half hour to fix the vacuum system. We'd spend the rest of the day in the water, snorkeling and sunbathing around Staniel Cay, just 15 minutes east of Compass Cay. Thunderball Cave, or Grotto is located between the two islands, but closer to Staniel. It was made famous by a James Bond movie called *Thunderball.* The underwater cavern accessible to snorkelers during low tide.

Jamie packed a cooler full of beer and a few leftover croissants, and I gathered the sunscreen and hats.

"This is one of the most beautiful diving spots in all of the Bahamas," Nick said as we geared up.

From the boat, the famous cave appeared to be a large limestone rock in the middle of the sea. Once in the water, even at low tide, the grotto looked menacing. It was hidden beneath waves crashing against the rocks. I followed the pack to the obscured entrance, adjusting my mask and fins along the way. Lucas grabbed my hand and yelled, "We are going to dive down briefly and emerge on the other side. Inside the cave."

"Okay" I said.

"Put your snorkel in your mouth and hold your breath."

I gave him the thumbs up, dutifully following his instructions. He held my hand through the rough entry, before we rapidly surfaced inside the grotto. We found a shallow rock where I could stand and remove my mask and snorkel. The natural skylight illuminated crystal clear water loaded with tropical fish. Yellow-striped angel fish, rainbow painted parrot fish and a tiny solitary orange and white spotted clown fish swam in-between the bright coral heads.

"Wow," I said.

"Let's swim around," Lucas suggested.

Jamie and Nick were already submerged, so I lowered my gear and placed my right hand in my lover's, allowing him to lead me around the grotto. The indigo glow highlighted Lucas's appearance underwater. His shoulders and chest seemed wider, so did his lips wrapped around the snorkel mouthpiece. His eyes appeared like a puffer fish when he looked over at me.

A crackling sound caught my attention, leading my gaze to a parrot fish below munching on coral. Everything else was sweetly silent. I felt something brush up against the back of my thigh, but looking back I spotted nothing. The Kramers appeared, signaling and taking pictures. Jamie pointed and waved, her eyes smiling through her mask. I swayed my hand back and forth, grinning tightly with the snorkel perched in my mouth. Lucas signaled me to surface with his thumb. I felt something on my thigh again and waved my hand back and forth over the intrusion.

Breaking the surface, I lifted my mask and spit out my snorkel. The three floated up along with two strangers. A twenty-something girl with short blond hair and a well-tanned slightly older guy with equally as bright sun-bleached hair, both sporting a mask and snorkel.

Jamie smiled widely and shouted, "A remora is trying to attach to the back of your thigh."

"What's a remora?" I asked.

"They attach to sharks." The petite blonde responded.

My eyes widened. "Does it think I'm a shark?"

Lucas laughed. "Probably."

"Seriously, is it still attached to me? And are they dangerous?"

The blonde briefly stuck her head in the water and quickly answered, "Yeah."

I froze. "Can someone get it off of me?" I asked in a high-pitched voice.

Everyone blankly gaped at me without action. "Just grab the damn thing and throw it off me."

"Raves, it's not dangerous. Kinda cool, really." Lucas said.

"Yeah, a good luck charm," Jamie chimed in.

"Well, it's not sucking on your leg. Grab it, and find a shark to stick it on."

Lucas dove down re-emerging and lifting-up a smiling remora. "Awe." The blonde exhaled.

Put it on the blonde, I thought. He disappeared again, resurfacing with a satisfied smile. "There's a nurse shark below. The two are happily re-united."

We all checked out the nurse and the attached remora and their clingy relationship. We did one last tour around the grotto, diving back into the sea to our anchored boat.

While underwater I recalled from Roman history and mythology, that a remora is associated with bringing down ships and had something to do with Mark Anthony's defeat at the Battle of Actium. I'm sure it's the same sucker fish.

I'll have to do an internet search later, I decided.

After devouring a few croissants back on the Intrepid, we headed to the neighboring Staniel Cay Yacht Club for a heartier meal. Several bright, round, cottages were nestled on the beach. The marina appeared lively, with a dozen or so boats tied up, and tropical music booming from the open-air pub. Several seagulls yapped, as I heard "mine, mine, mine-," instead from the cartoon *Finding Nemo*. A fried oily smell oozed from the restaurant.

An adorable Schnauzer-looking puppy rolled over and greeted us at the door. "How cute," I mumbled. Apparently, the dog liked this statement and rolled over again for a belly rub. I petted her for a few minutes and then joined the rest of the crew at the bar.

"Goombay Smashes for all," Jamie said, handing me one of the fruity cocktails.

"I'll drink to that," Nick agreed, raising his glass.

We ordered conch fritters, conch salad and French fries to split. The yacht club hummed with activity. Jamie disappeared to the outside swimming pool and the boys talked fishing with other fishermen sitting around the bar. I listened, occasionally shifting my attention outside to the cute puppy.

Nautical decor garnished the inside, a sea of boat flags dangling from the ceiling. It had a light and airy ambience. Windows lined three of the walls and opened screens allowed a subtle zephyr. Bar stools and a pool table comprised the main meeting hall, while framed photos of the filming of *Thunderball* covered another distant wall, and a few formal unoccupied tables sat apart from the others. Browsing the pictures, I recognized a young Sean Connery in a black suit posing with what appeared to be the filming crew.

A jovial middle-aged Bahamian bartender served us another round of Goombays. He had a contagious toothy smile. His near perfect opal whites could have easily been in a toothpaste commercial, especially contrasted against his chocolate skin. "Drink-up," he called out, placing four drinks in front of the three of us. "Plenty more, plenty more. You're in the islands, mon."

Jamie arrived, slightly wet, with a towel wrapped around her waist. The food appeared moments later. "Can we get a head of lettuce to go?" Jamie asked. "For the pigs."

"Pigs?" I asked, placidly.

She sat next to me and reached for a conch fritter. "Yes, swimming pigs. They live on a neighboring island and depend on tourists to feed them." She grabbed a bowl of conch salad and I mimicked her move, reaching for salad and a few fries. "They'll swim to the boat."

I took a sip of my drink. "I've never seen pigs swim. I'll bring them French fries."

"They eat anything," Lucas blurted.

"I've only seen pigs swimming on this island. Nick said. "It's a rarity. Rumor has it they were shipwrecked and the locals and tourists would bring them leftovers and food on the verge of spoiling. The pigs came to expect it, and would swim to approaching boats anticipating a meal." He snorted, "Last time we brought them popcorn, and they loved it."

"Oh." I paused, draining my glass of sweet fruity liquor. "I hope nobody brings them bacon, because it would just be wrong."

The three chuckled.

After lunch, Lucas and I stepped out to the veranda for a smoke. He bent down to rub the friendly Schnauzer's belly. "Whose dog is this anyway?" I asked the few tourists hanging around.

"Her name is Yoda, she's my baby." The girl with short blonde hair answered. She sat in a chair smoking, and I recognized her without the mask and snorkel.

"Well, she's a doll." I wasn't sure if she recognized me, free of the attached remora. I smiled before leaving for the Intrepid and our next adventure, feeding the famous swimming pigs.

Approaching the adjacent island, we saw a handful of boats congregated near the shoreline. I spotted five pigs in the water. A huge one grunted near a twenty-six-foot Contender, where teens handed her slices of bread from an oblong blue and yellow plastic bag. An older couple, perhaps in their early fifty's, floated next to the hogs taking pictures.

Jamie held a half-head of lettuce over the side of the boat and called out, "Here piggy, piggy."

I didn't know if lettuce would tempt the pig into approaching our boat. Perhaps popcorn would have been the better choice. After all, lettuce doesn't have much flavor without dressing. But sure enough, the large pig headed toward our Intrepid.

I started snapping photos. "That's Emily," Nick said. "The mama of the drove."

"Grab some lettuce Raves," Jamie called out. "The leftover fries are in the bag."

I chose a few fries, holding them over the port side, next to Jamie. Emily sucked down the treat in a nanosecond, her snout protruding from the sea. Waiting for more I seized the remaining portion, calling out to the boys, "Does anyone else want to feed the pig?"

"No." The guys replied. I heard a splash and spotted the two in the water, swimming toward Emily.

I pushed the bag in my hand toward Jamie. "Here, you feed her the rest."

She chortled, "You go ahead. You're the neophyte."

"You mean virgin?" I shot back with a grin.

Lucas emerged next to Emily, so I gave him a handful of fries to feed her, "Come swim with the pigs, honey." He urged, bouncing around the large swine.

I jumped into the calm water holding the remaining half head of lettuce. We swam around feeding the smaller hogs finding our way to the deserted beach, currently without inhabitants, but with plenty of evidence of tourists. Empty food containers and beer bottles littered the sand. "We should organize a clean-up day," I murmured.

"They already have one," Lucas said standing. "The locals from Staniel and some eco-friendly visitors clean it on a regular basis." He motioned me with his arm, "Come here." I followed him along the beach, wondering if he wanted another raw sexual encounter, unintentionally glancing back at the Kramers headed in the opposite direction. He led me to a scrub bush along the water line reciting a sing-song chant, "Here kitty-kitty."

"I'm right behind you," I hummed back.

He half laughed, continuing his chant while rattling a small bag. A handful of kittens emerged. Lucas glowed with affection at their timely appearance.

"What are you the pied-piper?" I asked. "Kittens don't just show up on abandoned islands when beckoned."

His lips turned into a slight smile, his eyes continued to glow. "They were here last time I came and the time before. It's a feral population." He opened a plastic bag exposing his treasure. "I brought them some fresh tuna and conch from the restaurant." He handed me some scraps, "They'll come to you. Just bend down and put out your hand."

"Floating pigs, wild cats…" I bent down as the shy felines approached. "Why don't they just eat the pigs? I think they'd like fresh ham or bacon."

He snickered, shaking his head with a dubious look.

"Just saying." I whispered. His tender fondness for the kittens warmed me, causing me to smile. We shared a love for nature, protecting and caring for creatures unable to care for themselves.

***

We spent the second half of the afternoon at leisure on Compass Cay. I had a quick shower, remaining make-up free, revealing a new carefree island side of me the past week with the exception of the evening at Atlantis. Alone on the bridge of *Cabin Fever*, I finished a few more chapters of the history based drug smuggling adventure. A thought about my drug stuffed idol dream triggered an impulsive giggle.

Giving my eyes a break, I decided to stroll the island trails, admiring the slow paced Bahamian way of life. Hakuna Matata came to mind, a phrase meaning no worries in Swahili. I was far away from Africa, yet the carefree approach to life seemed to fit more here than there. Kenya, Benin, South Africa and Egypt were all spectacular, yet a far cry from the tranquility of the Bahamas, islands holding quaint villages and marinas, similar yet each one slightly different. All had the same salty air, slow pace, and turquoise water, although the color varied. The people, both local and visitors changed. Compass Cay only had tourists, mostly extremely wealthy ones.

There wasn't an unnatural sound within earshot. Waves serenely collided with the sand and a slight wind tickled palm fronds. Not a single soul existed on the lee side of the island, just a ten minute walk from the already quiet Marina. I lit a cigarette and felt the warm sun soak my skin.

A hermit crab painted as a NASCAR crossed my path. "What the hell," I murmured.

Lucas appeared smiling widely and holding a lime-green painted hermit crab, sporting the number nine. "Would you like to race?"

I blinked a few times, "Sure." Us or the crabs?"

He placed number nine on the ground next to a red number thirteen. "Grab the red one and…" He drew two lines, a foot apart in the sand, pointing to each, "This is the starting point and this is the ending line."

Picking my lucky number thirteen, I lined up my racing pawn next to his. "For a five minute massage," I called out, poking my pawn past the starting point. They both walked in every direction but forward. Mine did a 360. I turned it in the correct direction, poked it, and then it climbed back into its shell rebelling against my techniques. Lucas's number nine slowly crawled in the opposite direction past the starting point.

"Well you have a homing pigeon. I guess I win by default," I concluded.

"You can't poke them, that's cheating." He looked at me with disbelief.

"I nudged it. Besides, I don't know the NASCAR hermit crab racing rules."

"How about a two minute shoulder massage, each?"

"Works for me," I gloated.

We sat on a solitary bench overlooking the peaceful Azul water, taking turns massaging. The crabs sat in the sand unmoved until we returned them to their NASCAR racing pen, housing ten other numbered shelled crustaceans. The sky was striped with cotton-candy pink cirrus clouds.

Strolling the docks, I admired a tall white heron intensely hunting in the shallow water. He had a bright yellow eye as if reflecting the sun itself. A few seagulls screamed cacaw as the water gently lapped. Nurse sharks navigated around, seemingly not disturbing the water-wading heron.

"I find beauty in the simplest places and simplest things," I confessed.

Approaching the Bluewater, I noticed a slight acrid scent tinged the air. "Smells like something electrical burning," Lucas addressed Nick as we boarded.

"Well, I've been smelling a faint smell, but it's getting stronger. I'm checking all the wires." The twosome walked over to the electrical box near the inside helm.

I popped up next to Jamie cooking in the galley. "What can I do?"

"The fish and rice are almost done. Could you make a salad?"

I whipped up a basic one comprised of lettuce, apples, cucumbers and almonds. "I smell it too, something burning. Are you worried?" I quizzed Jamie, looking for non-verbal signs of anxiety.

She had a tight smile, and answered in a toned down, uneasy voice. "It's not an emergency, but we have to address it during or after dinner. It's giving me a headache, and it's not normal."

I listened to Nick and Lucas vociferously checking the electrical box. "It's not the breakers," Nick said. "Check the bilge pump wires." They both scudded around through the main cabin. The acrid smell of burning increased, overpowering the fishy smell of dinner waiting. No visible smoke. Jamie opened the sliders and stuck her head out to breathe.

"Okay, here's the plan." Nick said loud enough for everyone on the island to hear. I stood attentive. "Let's eat dinner on the dock and discuss our next move." I guess I expected the Ten Commandments or a melodramatic proposal.

We all grabbed dishes and accoutrements, relocating them to a wooden picnic table. Jamie brought out two cocktails, handing her husband the largest cup. I imagined it full of rum to calm his nerves. Snatching a bottle of wine and two glasses, I filled both, passing one to my honey. All eyes focused on Nick. His sheer size and thunderous voice demanded attention when he acted as commander and chief.

He took a long gulp and breathed. "I don't trust this electrical system. None of us are electricians and something is definitely smoldering. I'm going to call the yacht club to see if they have any rooms for the night. Since they have more resources than Compass Cay, I'll feel more secure in their marina. Obviously we can't sleep on the yacht and I'm too old to sleep on the docks."

Jamie enthusiastically shook her head up and down in agreement. "Good plan, captain. I'm okay with camping, but a bed sounds much better."

Nick vanished and reappeared. She gave him a plate stacked with fish, rice and a small amount of salad. Tuning into what he said, the rest of us helped ourselves. He took a sip from his glass, directing his attention toward Lucas. "They have a bungalow available in Staniel. Email the company we chartered this boat from. Let them know what's going on, and ask if they have any idea about who we could have look at the electrical system. See if they can send the maintenance history. We don't even have manuals onboard."

Lucas nodded. "I have their email and phone number. I'll try both. It's late, but I'd like to leave a voice mail and an email, so they understand the urgency."

"Raven and Jamie, if you can get everything put away, then go with Lucas on the Intrepid. It's only twenty minutes, but you're safer there."

After dinner we scattered different directions. Both boats were untied and we were Staniel Cay bound within minutes.

CHAPTER NINE

MAY 31, 2011

STANIEL CAY

A two-story oceanfront bungalow awaited us. I packed an overnight bag with a few things we needed for the night. We lingered on the dock, securing boats and chatting with some local sail boaters, Oak and Larry from Georgia. Oak said, "The girls can stay with us," but Lucas, Jamie and I assured him we had nice accommodations waiting. He also guaranteed he'd keep an eye on the boats and nothing would catch fire or sink with him close-by. I wasn't so sure of his promise. Oak and Larry had been at sea for about five or six months, but they couldn't agree exactly how many. They had everything they needed, evidenced on their tattered, but overloaded sailboat. Even a pit-bull peacefully relaxed on their stained couch.

Our accommodations were as charming on the inside as they appeared to be on the exterior, which I admired from a distance during lunch earlier. We had the Ocean Blue Waterfront Suite with a balcony overhanging the sea. The Kramers took a spiral staircase to the queen bed on the second floor while Lucas and I were happy to sleep on the daybed in the living room. No wild sex for us tonight I assumed, since the cottage lacked privacy. I smiled at my deserted beach memory. I felt like we had the best view on the planet. The bungalow sat on stilts, with flood lights illuminating the turquoise water below. Two nurse shark shadows passed underneath. I looked forward to the view in the daytime or even at sunrise if I could drag myself out of bed early.

On the balcony, Lucas brought me a glass of Sauvignon Blanc. I lit a cigarette and inhaled. "Despite the boat problems, I'm having a wonderful time." I took a sip and tilted my head, "I hope everyone else is too?"

"Absolutely," he paused and lit a cigarette. "It's just as a captain, the responsibilities and safety of the vessel falls on you. Nick and I are both captains, so we need to make sure everyone is safe first and the boat doesn't catch on fire, and so forth." He took a drag and a sip of his absolute and cranberry. "I sent an email to the charter company. Electrical problems can be one of the most difficult to sort out. Nick's right, we're not electricians. I do have a friend who is an electrician, so I also sent him an email to see if he wants to join us in Staniel." He groaned and shook his head. "It just seems like one thing after another with this boat. The charter company should keep their vessels in tip-top shape."

"And you found this company how?"

"Online. It seemed like a good deal, and the Kramers also looked it over and agreed."

"Maybe it's not the boat, but my idol?" I teased.

He shot me a sideways look, "Bushwa."

I choked on my drink. "That doesn't sound like something from your vocabulary?"

He smiled wryly. "I learned it from Nick. It means nonsense."

I chuckled. "I know what it means. I just didn't expect to hear it from you."

His grinned widened, "I just happen to like the word."

"I think you like the bush part," I baited.

***

While sipping coffee prior to my morning routine, I watched two more sailboats arrive. Maybe they're Oak and Larry's friends from Georgia, I imagined. The Bluewater looked intact and the Kramers were milling about the dock. I attempted to sneak past the daybed holding my horizontal lover, but he grabbed my shorts, pulling me towards him. "And where do you think you're going?"

"Just to explore the island and see where my morning jog takes me." I fell over him crossing my body across his, face up. "The coffee is made and I even poured you a cup with cream and sugar." I stared at the ceiling, "And the boats look fine. The Kramers are on the dock and this means you're the last one out of bed."

"Oh, really." He wickedly grinned attempting to turn me over. I giggled and shot up.

"I need to go before the sun gets too intense."

I sashayed to the pool where the cute belly-rubbing loving mini-schnauzer greeted me. She rolled over for a tummy massage. I bent down, "Where's your mama, Yoda?"

Her eyes sparkled and tail wagged. I spotted the bubbly blonde near the outdoor shower and waved. "Good morning."

She waved back. I headed south on a dirt road which wound east then south again, passing golf carts, an airport, Bonefish Creek and private houses, for the most part unoccupied. Most of the homes I assumed belonged to Americans or other foreigners. They were well kept, but quiet at the moment. A plane landed as I crossed back over and around the airport. I stopped to watch the small Cessna do a go-around then land safely. The runway appeared short, ending at the waterline. *I'll have to check out the landing strip,* I made a mental note, wondering if a plane or two rested in the shallow waters like Norman's Cay.

On a hill closer to the Yacht Club sat a cluster of local Bahamian homes. They were smaller and basic, but colorful with more activity. Some doors were open, a baby cried, a TV blared and on one porch, two men played dominos. I jumped into the pool at the end of my four-mile jog, cooling my sweat-soaked salty skin. I finished with an outside shower soap-up and rinse through my running bra and shorts.

At a picnic table on the dock, Lucas got me up to speed on the latest developments. *Cabin Fever* still had an electrical problem. He read me the response of the charter company, Windstar, from his laptop.

The Bluewater was donated from a church with no records of the boats previous maintenance. It's a new charter, and you are the first to rent this vessel. Our team examined *Cabin Fever* prior to your rental. It passed a rigorous inspection. It's your responsibility to return the yacht to Miami as the signed contract states. If you are unable to do so, we need to know ASAP.

He guffawed. "And here's my response." He continued reading.

You were very much aware I planned on taking the boat to the Bahamas. I'm in the boat business and I know typical things that can go wrong with a vessel. Weather, toilets and other things we experienced. However, an electrical fire or possible bilge pump failure is over the top. I'll get *Cabin Fever* back to Miami. At my own expense, I'm flying in a friend who's an electrician for troubleshooting. You should have let me know it was a donation and has no history with your company. I expect a credit for spending valuable time and money on a boat with no records or history. You don't even know if this vessel has sunk at some point, which would explain a lot. This is now a liability issue. I intend on getting it back to the states as soon as I am able to do so.

"Ouch," I mumbled. "Well, you told them. Besides, they weren't honest from the beginning. They should've told you it lacks provenience or a proven record and really shouldn't be in their fleet, except for maybe as a local rental."

He exhaled in disbelief. "Yeah. Well, my friend Russ is flying into Staniel today. Hopefully, he can figure it out. I told him I'd pay for his vacation, flight and so forth. He loves the islands.

"I'd love to see the airport. I ran by it during my exploration. I watched a Cessna 182 do a go-around and…"

Jamie materialized on the dock extending her hand, offering a plate of orange muffins. Lucas snatched a muffin, wandering off with his laptop. I picked a small one. "Thanks. You were cooking in there, with that pungent smell?"

"It's getting better, with all the windows open. I can take it in small doses with lots of deck breaks while they're baking. We already had breakfast, and I thought you might be hungry after your run."

I took a bite, "Excellent. You're amazing." Although lacking in the domestication department, I enjoyed cooking, even though I rarely did it myself. "So yummy," I mumbled finishing up in a few large nibbles.

Jamie beamed at my satisfaction. "We rented a golf cart for the afternoon," she hummed. "I'm going to catch a few rays poolside."

I nodded. "I'll see you there in a bit."

Walking off, I scouted the docks for Lucas. I spotted him talking to a few guys near the fish cleaning station. Nick checked out a large European yacht at the opposite end of the marina. I recognized it as an Azimut, from the three distinct windows on the side and its aerodynamic design. One of the few boats I could spot and identify, it was also my dream boat. This one was curiously named *Davy Jones*. Was the owner one of the band members from *The Monkees?* In my youth, I loved watching the TV show and listening to the pop group. Or is it a reference to Davy Jones Locker, the bottom of the sea?

I strolled over to my honey. Nurse sharks swarmed below in a feeding frenzy, attacking like Komodo Dragons on raw meat. They didn't look so peaceful or harmless now.

Lucas noticed me standing by his side. "Hey, sweetie." He turned to one of the guys fileting fish, "This is my girlfriend Raves."

The tall, thin, shirtless stranger greeted me with a nod, "Nice to meet you." He glanced up from the fish he skinned. "I'd shake your hand, but they're a bit bloody right now." Two large fish were splayed on the filet table and a bucket full of fresh meat lay between his feet. He wore plastic blue fishing waders. "I'm Paul, and this is my buddy Randy." I smiled at the younger, less messy fisherman. His fish scraps seamlessly fell from the table into the shark infested water. He was barefoot, wearing only a bathing suit and a knife attached to his calf.

"Dolphinfish?" I asked, with my newfound yet limited fishing lingo.

"Yes Ma'am," Paul answered in a long drawl. "Got a few at sunrise, just out yonder."

Lucas chimed in, "They're from Fort Lauderdale."

I thought his accent sounded a bit country-strong for southern Florida. "Neighbors." I offered without expectation while peering into the sea at the bloodbath. My eyes drifted toward Lucas. "I'm going poolside until we leave on the golf cart."

"We're leaving in forty-three minutes."

Where does he get these numbers? I thought, but simply nodded. *Not forty or forty-five. So random, yet totally his personality. Mostly normal but a little off, organized chaos perhaps.* I headed for the pool.

Jamie, the blonde, and her pup Yoda were all sunbathing at the small pool. "What are you drinking?" I called out, half expecting a water or soda.

"Pina colada," Jamie responded.

I checked my watch and returned with two fresh drinks and a small bowl of ice water for the dog. "I brought some water for

Yoda, if you don't mind?" I placed the ceramic dish on the ground.

"Ahh, thanks. I've been giving her ice cubes from my drink and she swims in the pool."

"She's such a cutie." I sat in the lounge chair between Jamie, who was immersed in a magazine, and the blonde. "And a good traveler?" I added after a quick sip from my sweet cocktail.

She beamed. "Yes, I've only had her for about nine months. But she goes everywhere with me."

"Where do you call home?"

"North Carolina, but we've been traveling for the past few years on our boat." She paused, sitting more erect. "I'm Jenny, here with my husband, it's our fifth anniversary."

"Congrats on five years. I'm Raves." I raised my pina colada to her unknown cocktail. She lit a cigarette and I borrowed one.

"You smoke? I thought I saw you running."

"Yes, I do both." I mumbled, not really wanting to explain my bipolar tendencies yet again.

She giggled with a knowing grin. "No worries."

I glanced at Jamie. Yoda rested in the shade under her lounge chair. I imagined the pup having a punky attitude. Confident, smart, somewhat rebellious and spoiled. "So you're sailing around the Bahamas?" I probed.

"Yeah." She pointed to the marina. "Our boat is docked over there for the next week. It's called *Davy Jones.*"

My eyes widened through my sunglasses. I'd assumed she was on one of the many sailboats. "An Azimut. My favorite." I took a sip, "And is your husband Davy?"

She giggled. "No, he's Jeff Johnson." She extinguished her cigarette into her empty glass. "He's a treasure hunter looking for Spanish shipwrecks, mostly in the Bahamas." She clarified. "He does web design and hosting for a living, but his passion is treasure hunting."

"What type of treasure has he found? I asked.

"He's obsessed with a certain idol he thinks is located in the Bahamas. He thinks it holds magical powers. He's been searching for it for years, and has found some cool stuff in the process. Cannons, and a few pieces of eight and…"

"What type of statue? I interrupted, asking in a tightened high voice. I felt paralyzed, short of breath, suddenly convinced he was looking for my idol. Sensing my anxiety, Yoda jumped on my lap, licking my calf.

Jamie lowered her sunglasses and whispered, "I heard what she said. You're as pale as a ghost and I know what you're thinking. Breathe. Just breathe. I'm sure he's not looking for Uga-Bugga. Thousands of statues exist in this area."

Jenny handed her phone to me. "I sketched this rendering of the statue based on Jeff's description, and this is a picture of it. No photos exist. It's based on historical descriptions and lore."

I studied the photo. It appeared fiercer looking than my idol, more warrior-like. The eyes were noticeably larger and oval shaped. He had a long drawn-out nose with flaring nostrils, small pouty lips and a square chiseled chin. His cheekbones were more pronounced, and his chest and legs more muscular. A loincloth covered his private parts and he carried a large spear, or more-like a trident.

"What's the idol believed to be made of and from?" I asked, looking for a greater similarity between her portrait and Uga-Bugga. After all, her rendition is based on second or even third hand information.

"Crystal, from what I understand. There are lots of different accounts of where it's from. Jeff thinks it's in the Bahamas from a few written accounts back in the 1700's. I drew him holding a trident because it's believed to bring down sailors and rule the sea." She giggled. "It's my rendition and I thought a trident was appropriate."

I smiled, handing her phone back. "It's a nice drawing and you're a good artist." Jenny seemed innocent enough, but I didn't trust treasure hunters. My intuition urged me to be careful around the two. "We're going to change for our island exploration. See you later this afternoon, I hope."

"I think Yoda likes you Raves," she uttered.

I rose and placed a quick peck of gratitude on Yoda's head for the puppy kisses. "Yoda is such a cute name. How did you pick it?" I asked, hoping it wasn't some omen or occultation of an otherwise innocent moniker.

"Oh, we're Star Wars fans."

I calmed at the response. *Great, the Star Wars Jedi master meets the sea devil.* Following Jamie to the cottage, I imagined the dog and a horned demon dueling it out with light sabers to save the galaxy. Somehow in my mind's eye, the adorable pup won the battle before I even reached the doorstep.

The guys were waiting, ready to sightsee, "Has it been forty-three minutes?" I called out to Lucas.

"Forty-four," he taunted.

We sauntered to the golf cart with no plans but to be at the airport around 3:00 or whenever we saw the Caravan fly overhead. I wanted to stop by a local grocery store and Jamie was seeking boutiques. We wore our bathing suits with cover-ups. Jamie and I rode on the back of the four-seater with the boys navigating in the front. Crossing the rickety bridge over Bonefish Creek, Lucas decided to stop and admire the fleeting fish. A Piper Aztec buzzed us. "Not a Caravan," he announced.

A small market sat across from the creek. "Can we check out the local grocer?" I pointed to a coral shack while removing a shawl draped over my shoulders.

We pulled in and Jamie and I jumped off the cart. I perused the can goods and cereal boxes. There was plenty of beans, rice, oatmeal and a few boxes of Captain Crunch and Cheerios. The elderly Bahamian lady watched me like a bird stalking its prey.

"My God. You can't come in here without a shirt," she chided.

"Oh, I didn't know. Sorry," I murmured, feeling uncharacteristically awkward. I usually followed the cultural norm, but the islands seemed so casual and swimsuit savvy. It's not like I entered a church or a temple half-naked. Although nowadays, it's probably been done.

Exiting the shack, I noticed Jamie still wearing her cover-up. Behind me she carried four opened Kalik lights. "I don't think she liked your cleavage," she kidded. "What are you like a 36D?"

"C," I corrected. "It's the islands. Who knew?"

Following the same dirt road, I jogged on just hours prior, at the fork in the road we veered the opposite direction. Revealing more tropical houses, some landscaped, others barren like a desert covered in sand lacking anything lush, leafy or remotely fertile. Easy to care for, I assumed. Some homes had the native sea-grape bushes I recognized as a staple on the islands. A rare grass patch appeared in front of a two-storied home perched on stilts sheltering a trailered thirty-nine-foot center console under its belly. We stopped to check out the make and model.

"A Yellowfin," Lucas announced, resuming our leisurely ride.

"Hey Raves, did you tell Lucas about the *Davy Jones* boat?"

"I met the owner, Jeff." Nick said. "Nice guy."

"Well, we met his wife and dog at the pool. Jeff's a treasure hunter and he's searching for an idol in the Bahamas. I don't think it's a coincidence. What I found on the beach in Bimini might be what he is desperately seeking. And I don't like his boat name, it means death to sailors. Besides my intuition is screaming at me to stay away from this guy."

The threesome snickered, with Lucas degenerating into a lingering belly laugh.

I blinked at him, raising my lips slightly. "Do you even know what Davy Jones means, sweetie?"

He answered with amusement, "Yes. Sponge Bob had a locker at the bottom of the ocean where he keeps his socks." He belly-laughed again, abruptly stopping the cart.

Nick spoke through his smile, glancing back at me. "He's a treasure hunter, I think the name is appropriate. Just ask him about the idol he is seeking, I doubt it's the same one."

"Jenny showed me a picture she drew of it, and explained its lore briefly."

"And?" Nick asked.

"It doesn't really look like Uga-Bugga, but it's not completely dissimilar. It's made of a powerful crystal and it's believed to cause terror at sea."

"You two should have a lot in common. I'll introduce you tonight," Nick said.

We meandered along the dirt road, finding ourselves at a secluded lagoon. Jamie rushed into the shallow cerulean calm water waving her hands and shouting into the air, "Come join me."

The boys dove into the crystal clear water. I blissfully sat my butt in the sand allowing the gentle waves touch my feet. I laid back into my palms, soaking up the sun. Seagulls squawked, waves purred and the faint sound of my friends hummed in the distance.

Life is beautiful and so is this island, I reflected. *I could spend years at sea, like Jenny and Jeff.* Perhaps I'd overanalyzed Jeff's idol search and let my imagination run wild. If the statue he pursued was made of wood, then I'd have no doubt about it. But crystal? Amongst the surrounding beauty Jimmy Buffett played in my head, *changes in attitude, changes in latitude.* A low flying plane buzzed overhead, interrupting Buffett's trendy song in my mind.

"That's the caravan," Lucas hollered. "Let's get to the airport."

We took a seven minute cart ride to the landing strip, arriving as the caravan taxied to a cemented square in front of a large hanger. Two Cessna's and a Cirrus were tied down on one side, all three half the size of the new arrival. The pilot and three passengers disembarked.

A man appearing to be in his late forties approached our golf cart. He looked slightly smaller and stockier than the two men in our group, sporting worn jeans, a plain white t-shirt, a cowboy hat and boots. Extending his hand to Lucas, he said "Howdy old friend."

He firmly shook and then motioned towards us. "Hey Russ. This is my girlfriend Raves and my friends, Jamie and Nick."

"Howdy," he nodded. "Can I squeeze between the two girls on the back of the golf cart?"

"I can walk," I offered. "It's only five minutes."

"Non-sense." He said, emphasizing the "Non" part of the word with a slight drawl on the latter. "I'll just stand on the back. Besides, I like the view."

"Can I put your backpack on my lap?"

"Yes ma'am, if you don't mind."

Within minutes we were lunching at the yacht club, discussing problems we encountered on the Bluewater. Cowboy removed his hat and to my surprise revealed a full black head of hair, wavy and naturally smoothed back from his face. He had a strong jaw with a day's worth of salt and pepper stubble, barely noticeable. He placed his hat on the empty seat next to him. His eyes appeared amber, almond-shaped and slightly sensual, radiating an experienced confidence.

"It sounds like quite the rodeo," he wryly said. He had a minor southern accent, barely recognizable except his words were more pronounced and prolonged.

"That's not all," Lucas sputtered. "Raven holds an artifact she thinks is cursed."

His eyebrows lifted in amusement. "I can fix electrical problems, but not curses."

Discussion of the idol ensued over fresh sushi, French fries and much teasing.

"Doesn't Raven mean bad luck?" Russ asked.

Nick added, "I think you're right. Ravens show up just before evil occurs."

"Funny, funny boys. It's Native American, not Hollywood lore. A Raven is the bringer of light, not darkness."

The group separated, the three men sauntering off to assess the Bluewater quandary. Jamie disappeared to the cottage and I hung out in the bar drinking a Goombay Smash with Jenny and Jeff. I didn't have any desire to do anything or be anywhere, becoming accustomed to island time and the laid back lifestyle.

In the distance I noticed a small boat with two Bahamians, one on the back near the engine, one standing on the bow with a rope preparing to tie up to the dock. Fishermen selling their fish or conch to the Yacht Club, I guessed. Beyond them, two boats drifted around *Thunderball* Cave. I wondered if the remora attached to another unsuspecting tourist, my lips turning upwards at the thought.

I invited Jeff into a conversation for the first time, "So what kind of treasures have you found under the sea?" I said, hoping he'd offer information about his search for the statue.

His ice blue eyes lit-up. "My best finds were off the coast of Florida, from the 1715 Spanish Fleet that got wiped out from a hurricane. I've found quite a few pieces of eight, cannons, Chinese porcelain, various silver objects and the like. A few gold pieces, but not the mother-lode."

His sunbathed blond curls framed his face, pausing momentarily for a sip of his cocktail and a cigarette. I followed his lead, listening intently. "I used to work with the Fishers. You know, Mel Fishers group discovered the famed *Atocha*." I nodded. "We had a disagreement and went our separate ways. I stay away from their areas now. In fact, I'm more interested in the Bahamas and the undiscovered shipwrecks here."

"The Bahamian government allows you to work here?" I inquired.

He smiled shrewdly, exposing small teeth prior to taking a deep inhale of smoke. "I'm not working here. Just checking things out."

Tell that to your wife broadcasting to me, a complete stranger, that you're treasure hunting and searching for a specific idol, I thought, noticing for the first time she no longer sat next to him.

I quickly corrected my judgment. "I mean I know the salvage laws are different here in the Bahamas. Florida allows exploration with a permit. The State takes twenty percent, allowing the divers to keep the rest." I hesitated. "But from what I understand, treasure hunting in the Bahamas is illegal or permits are at least rare. Right?"

His eyes widened and he seemed a bit taken back.

"I'm an archaeologist, I explained. I work at a museum now, but I know quite a bit about recovery and shipwrecks. However, I never worked underwater, just on land excavations."

"Get out of here. I've worked with archaeologists, mostly male. Some of them don't like us you know. Treasure hunters have a bad reputation among academics."

I smiled. "Rightfully so, but I think it's changing." I took a sip of my Goombay. "Many of these guys don't record anything. They just pillage like pirates. But others do the right thing, documenting and revealing all the artifacts they discover. I'm sure you fall in the latter category," I winked.

His sly grin returned. "I do my best. What museum do you work at?"

"The Graves," realizing for the first time how deadly it sounded. "I'm the education director. I have the summer off." I turned the attention back to his finds, prodding deeper for information about his search. "The 1715 fleet is highly sought after, so why would you abandon such a hot area for the Bahamas?"

"That's exactly why I left. Too many treasure hunters, all lying and cheating each other. You don't know who to trust. There are false claims and information, illegal looting and problems with permits. The area has been thoroughly picked over and exploited since the 60's. Every wannabe is jumping in with metal detectors, thinking they're the next Mel Fisher looking to strike it rich. The truth is, the water is dirty with horrible visibility. If there is an undiscovered shipwreck there the odds of finding it without the right equipment are very unlikely."

I drained my glass, signaling the bartender for two more. "Out of the eleven how many have been identified?"

"Four for sure, but probably five. One made it back to Spain and the others are still undiscovered. It's controversial. Many books have been written about the fleet, with various speculations."

"From what I recall they left Havana in July of 1715 loaded with the Queen's Jewels and an unusually high amount of treasure from the New World because the fleet hadn't been able to return for four years due to the Spanish War. When the war ended the crown sent for the fleet to return immediately because Spain needed the money. They hugged the Florida coastline with the intention of reaching St. Augustine before starting the crossing. A category 5 hurricane hit, and smashed the fleet into the shallow water and shores somewhere around Fort Pierce to Sebastian area." I scanned his face for a reaction.

He smirked. "That pretty much sums it up. Let's toast the 1715 fleet." Our refilled Goombays sat on the countertop, we clicked plastic cups to the occasion.

I guess I had to take a more direct approach. "Just one more thing. Jenny said you are searching for an idol. Is it related to the Queen's Jewels?"

"Ah, my whimsical wife. Sometimes she exaggerates and has an overactive imagination. I am interested in an idol I believe exists. While working the 1715 wrecks I did quite a bit of research. I even went to Havana to copy some documents in their library. A carved crystal statue sailed with the fleet. The locals firmly believed it had magical powers for both healing and destruction." He took a swig from his glass. "I'm very interested in this idol, but I wouldn't consider myself searching for it. That'd be a crap shoot in this vast ocean."

"Why do you think it's in the Bahamas?"

"Call it a hunch. There've been many reports of a green glow from various locations around the islands. At times, the statue is reported to radiate a luminous green light. Sailors reported seeing it for miles according to historical documents in Havana. The past few years I've heard of a few reports from the Bahamas."

"How large is it?"

"One account puts it around a few feet tall."

It's the same size as mine, I thought. *But Uga-Bugga looks different and is made of wood.* I still wasn't taking the chance.

"I overheard your friends teasing you about a cursed idol." Jeff took a long gulp from his drink. "Can I see it?"

"Oh, it's nothing like the one you're looking for. It's just a voodoo doll." I said, hoping he'd lose interest.

"I'd love to see it. I have some experience with African dolls."

"Meet me at *Cabin Fever* in five minutes." I was buying time. With two boats and a cottage, I didn't want him to know where I kept it. Perhaps I seemed paranoid, but I trusted my intuition.

I walked quickly past Russ and Lucas troubleshooting the boat, so they didn't notice me enter the cabin. The ship was unplugged from the electricity and all doors and windows were open, allowing in natural light and fresh air. It smelled as if someone sprayed lemon-scented glade. I retrieved my idol from under the bed. It radiated heat, so I placed it in the freezer for a few minutes.

"Raven." I heard Jeff call from the dock.

I grabbed the idol from the freezer and placed it on the counter, it had slightly cooled. "Come in Jeff."

He walked towards me, casually looking around the cabin. I found myself slightly nervous.

"Electrical problems," I explained. "The guys are trying to fix the problem now. Would you like a beer?"

"This must be the cursed idol." He said, standing next to me as I handed him a beer and opened one for myself.

"I call it Uga-Bugga" I held it up. "See, it looks like an African voodoo doll. It's why my friends tease me about it being cursed." I said, scanning his face for a reaction. He seemed unmoved. I didn't want to share my nightmares or the misfortunes we'd encountered at sea.

He held out his hand. "Can I hold it?"

I hesitated, and then watchfully placed it in his hand.

"Where did you find it?"

"On the beach in Bimini." I said, leaning against the kitchen counter.

"Huh." He rotated the statue checking out all angles.

From the corner of my eye, I noticed Russ examining the electrical distribution center in the salon, still wearing his boots but not his hat. "It also reminds me of Ashanti fertility dolls from the Ivory Coast, but the head is completely different. Their statues have flat heads, however, the genitals are pronounced, almost a focal point in the Ashanti dolls, like this statue."

He blushed a baby pink. An unexpected response from a treasure hunter. I watched his facial features for an indication of his thoughts.

"It does remind me of some figurines I've seen in Namibia, Africa while looking for a Spanish shipwreck there." I could see him searching his mind. "The statues were in a small museum. The features, size and material of this piece are similar." He examined the top of its head, slowly rubbing the circular cavity.

I felt my body relax. "So you think it's African?" I asked.

Russ turned around, offering his opinion, "Isn't Atlantis supposedly in Bimini, the so called Bimini Road? I mean I'm not an expert, but since you found it right there. Could it be like a portal between Africa and the Bahamas? He snatched a beer from the fridge. "Anybody want one?"

"We're good." I sipped my beer, and Jeff barely touched his. I was talking about the lost city of Atlantis and portals with a cowboy and treasure hunter. If Atlantis did exist, I believed it wouldn't be found in the Americas.

Nick rushed into the cabin panting, looking uncharacteristically frazzled. "Where's Lucas, I have a problem...an emergency. I need to talk to him."

I bolted to the aft of the boat, calling his name as I went, locating him in the engine room, untangling wires. "Hey, Nick needs you right away. He said it's an emergency."

Within minutes we were standing in front of him, as he paced with Jamie by his side.

"I just got a phone call from the Vice President of Exxon. There's been an oil rig explosion. Oil is gushing into the Gulf of Mexico. They're airlifting crew off the rig right now, but lives have been lost. I need to get back to Texas ASAP. My Dassault Falcon, is currently en route from Corpus Christi to Miami."

"What do you need me to do?" Lucas asked, all eyes still on Nick.

"I need to get to Miami. The jet can't land here with such a short runway." He paused. "I need to see if any flights are going out."

"Watermakers is the only scheduled flight, and it just took off after Russ arrived. I can call my flight instructor and see if he can bring our plane," Lucas offered.

"It's worth a shot."

Lucas made a few phone calls. Jeff handed the statue back to me and said he'd talk to the yacht club owner about other flights. Russ went back to troubleshooting electrical problems, while the rest of us waited. I stuck the idol back in the freezer, its temporary hiding spot.

"My instructor didn't answer, so I left a message. We need to think about plan B, since it's a two hour flight in our Cessna each way." Lucas checked his watch, pausing and searching for a resolution. I pictured his thoughts whirling at tornadic speeds. "It's a four hour boat ride to Nassau in the Intrepid. They have more flights available, but it's already almost 5:00."

"Let's go to the airport and see what planes are there. I remember seeing a few on the tarmac, if we can find an owner, they might be convinced to take me." Nick said, quickly turning to his wife. "Darling, can you pack a bag of what we absolutely need. Including passports?"

Jamie hurried off and the three of us walked through the bar, catching up with Jeff talking to the club owner. The rig explosion was the top story on CNN. Nick interrupted the two men, "Sorry. But do you know who owns any of the planes at the airport?"

"I was just telling your friend I'm expecting a couple of people arriving very shortly on a charter flight. The plane is called a yellow taxi, and he's just dropping them off and then returning to Florida."

Nick's eyes sparked. "Thanks. Let's go. Raven, can you tell Jamie to hurry. We'll be on the cart."

I ran to bungalow calling out, "You might have a flight. They're waiting for us on the golf cart."

She rushed with just her purse and a small duffle bag. "Raves can you put everything I left here back on the boat before you guys leave the resort?"

"Of course."

"This is disappointing," she confessed. "It's going to be a circus with the media back in Texas."

"You're handling it well. You need to be an anchor for your husband right now, and I think you seem solid as a rock."

"Thanks." We leaped onto the rear of the golf cart, Lucas driving full speed. She fumbled around the interior of her purse, pulling out a piece of paper and handing it to me. "Here's my email and phone number, I want to know what happens with the boat, idol and everything else. Promise me you'll examine your nightmares and lack of childhood memories."

Taken back, I nervously chuckled. "Will do."

CHAPTER TEN

MAY 31, 2011

STANIEL CAY

I walked slowly around the docks, a bit sullen about the Kramers leaving. I really adored the couple, with Nick's stories about the history of the islands and Jamie perpetually humming and cooking. I'd grown attached to the two of them in only a few days. I must have appeared bummed wandering past Oak near his sailboat.

"What's the sad face for, honey?"

I looked up, "Oh, I'm fine. My friends just left, but I'll get over it."

He extended the palm of his hand, revealing a rolled joint. "A little Maui Wowie can cure your woes."

I half giggled. "Oh, thanks. I'm good."

He lit the cigarette-sized joint, inhaled, and then pushed it towards me. "No, really, I'm fine."

He blew the smoke in my direction, "How about a beer then?"

My lips ruefully turned upwards, "Sounds good."

He inhaled again, then called out to Larry on the boat, "Can you hand me a beer for this little darling?"

Larry peeked out and then handed me a can of Natural Light,

quickly retreating back into his shell like a frightened turtle. "What's his deal?" I heard myself ask.

A cloud of sweet marijuana hit my nostrils as Oak puffed away. I noticed for the first time a string of red Christmas lights surrounding the rails and boom of the boat. Their own personal red light district, I imagined. "Larry just likes to get stoned and watch movies during the day," Oak exhaled. I cracked a smile. "And I smoke for medical reasons," he shared. "I have back problems and my legs get numb sometimes."

"Oh, no worries. I think it should be legal, it's just not for me."

Oak continued to share his medical history as well as views on politics and drugs. I half-listened, kicking my feet around while studying his overloaded sailboat. Red, blue and yellow jugs lined the rails. The red held fuel and blue one water I envisioned, but the yellow ones were a mystery. Tattered clothes and towels were thrown over one banister, below those rested a plastic green canoe side-strapped with an overabundance of bungee cords. A confederate flag swayed from the mast alongside a Bahamian one. Swiveling from the port side a UFO shaped grill teetered in the gentle wind, while a larger grill sat on the stern, bordering several heavy-duty grey containers and brass-stained coolers. My mind contemplated their contents, and I did a double take on the name of the boat, *Hillbilly Express*.

I heard Lucas calling me from the Bluewater. "Thanks for the beer," I said. Although a pretty foul-tasting one, the interaction with Oak warmed my spirits.

The yacht lacked the low hum I was accustomed to hearing. I joined the two guys sitting on the couch engaged in conversation. Russ still wore his jeans and cowboy boots, his hands dirty and battered looking. Lucas sat shirtless in a swimsuit. He had some hand scuffs, but none as noticeable as Russ's.

"Well, we have a temporary fix," Russ said, glancing at me then Lucas. "We need to get this boat back to the states." He paused. "I disconnected some problematic wires leaving us with limited power. We'll only have power when docked in the harbor, at night when needed. Lucas, we need the fastest route.

"Nassau, Bimini to Miami is the shortest and easiest." He said. "At a cruise speed of eight to ten knots."

"I thought so." Russ agreed. "The boat seems safe en route and while docked."

"Let's sleep in the cottage tonight. I've already paid." Lucas said.

"Now lighten up, y'all." Russ smiled. "Let's have some fun. The boat will be fine. Besides, we have the Intrepid." He shook his head, "I've just never seen so many messed up wires, miss-labeled, going to strange places, all rigged out and reassembled. So plug in your phones, laptops and such tonight in the hut."

I grabbed my laptop and idol suddenly realizing all our frozen and cold food would go bad. "Uh, what about the fridge and freezer?"

"Just don't open them too much and it'll be fine. Raves haven't you ever been through a hurricane?" Russ asked.

"Um, no."

He poured himself a rum and coke, minus the ice. "We'll have plenty of bags of ice in the cooler. And there's a strong organized tropical wave out there, really early in the season. So you may have your chance to experience one."

"What?" Lucas disbelievingly shot back.

"I saw it on the weather channel this morning," he calmly answered.

I placed my idol wrapped in a beach towel on top of the laptop and sauntered back to the bungalow. I needed to check email and do some online research for the first time since Andros. I googled, *are portals real?* I came up with numerous websites and clicked on a NASA link. According to the website magnetic portals are real and open and close dozens of times a day, usually without warning. NASA developed ways to find some portals, and the website went into a complex scientific explanation.

So did a portal spit out my idol or the foot-scratching mischievous spirit? Is it just happenstance? Could they detect a portal around Bimini? I wondered.

I scrolled down my results and clicked on another link, less scientific and more paranormal. This site described how I could find one by holding a pre-programmed crystal and if it vibrated and warmed immensely, then there was a portal present. It also warned of not opening and closing portals unless you know what you're doing. I imagined most people wouldn't, including me.

Next I googled *African idol, wood statues, pics of wooden statues* and finally *African fertility dolls.* None of the images resembled Uga-Bugga, however information concerning the use of fertility figures in Africa was noteworthy. During my search several links for

Voodoo dolls appeared, so I clicked on one.

Invented in Africa, real voodoo dolls are extremely powerful. They are divided into two categories, good and destroyer. The good ones will drive away evil spirits and protect you while the destroyer will work against your enemies and make them suffer.

I clicked on another Voodoo website. *One does not choose Voodoo, it chooses you.* Oh great, what did I get myself into? Is Uga-Bugga a voodoo doll? Did a spirit attach itself to me while I attended the ceremony in Benin?

Although I was on Wi-Fi, the internet seemed painfully slow. A headshot photo of Nick's flashed across my screen with a statement underneath reading, *"The oil disaster is being examined. We will make right by this tragedy."* He looked handsome and CEO worthy in a suit and tie, only visible from the shoulders up. He must have conducted a phone interview as soon as he landed. *There goes his Falcon,* I thought, sending Jamie a brief message letting her know I enjoyed our time together and I hoped she patiently handled the chaos surrounding the explosion and ensuing oil spill. I closed my laptop and stepped onto the balcony for a cigarette.

Country music blared from the docks, and nurse sharks gathered for an evening feast of fish scraps cascading into the Atlantic. A pelican swooped, braving the shark filled waters for a piece of the action. Swift and fearless, it caught a scrap midair, not even giving the nurses a chance. The sharks swam on top of one another in a chockablock heap. The pelican did a go-around, returning this time with a few friends. I recognized familiar faces surrounding the fish cleaning station, including Jenny, Jeff, Russ and Lucas.

Russ must have noticed me, calling up to the balcony, "Come join us for sushi Raves."

I smiled, nodded and waved, shouting, "Okay."

Emerging below, I realized the music came from our Intrepid, Russ' choice, I concluded. Fileted tuna spread across a wooden picnic table with soy sauce and wasabi. The smell of burgers soured the salubrious air. I munched wasabi drenched yellowfin, numbing my senses with the intense burn. Inhaling the brief pain, I turned towards Russ, who was arranging hamburgers on the public grill, "So do you always wear cowboy boots?"

"No Ma'am," his grinned widened. "Just for my flight here. I brought shorts and flip-flops for the rest of the trip, but I'm always prepared for a rodeo."

"We definitely have some sort of rodeo going on. Maybe a little different from what you're used to."

He snickered and shook the ice against his otherwise empty glass. "It's all good. Hell, we're in Paradise." Handing me his glass, he asked, "Would you mind getting me a rum and coke, some buns...and all the burger fixings?"

"Sure." I walked past the cloud of smoke encircling the *Hillbilly Express,* returning with a few drinks, a soy burger wrapped in foil, and all the accoutrements. I threw my foiled veggie burger on the crowded grill. Yoda patiently sat next to Russ, her nose wiggling in the meaty air.

"What's that?" Russ asked.

"A soy burger," I nonchalantly answered. "I'm a pescatarian. I don't eat any meat except fish and seafood."

He shook his head, "I've never heard of such a thing. It sounds like an occupation, not a way of eating."

I smiled widely, giggling. "Well, now you have. It's basically a vegetarian who eats fish."

"If you say so." He placed the hamburgers on buns, leaving mine on the hot grill. "So, I'll leave you in charge of the soy disk, since I'm clueless how to tell when it's done." He walked off, burger in hand towards the other fishermen congregating near the cleaning station.

It was happy-hour on the dock. Newfound friends meandered by, swooping up sushi and burgers, like the pelicans I'd watched earlier. Yoda ate every scrap hitting the ground, spotting an airborne crumb as if it was a missile, occasionally snapping at a fly. Small talk buzzed around the now tropical storm brewing in the Caribbean and the deadly oil spill. Apparently, this storm was one of the earliest ones on record. I kept my mouth zipped about our friend's oil spill involvement. Many of the anglers were environmentally conscious and although the Kramers had nothing to do with the tragedy, just being associated with the company responsible for such a disaster might make them unfavorably judged. The oil already killed fish and wildlife in the Gulf and had long-term effects on the entire ecosystem.

Jeff stopped by for a burger. "What do you plan on doing with your statue?"

"I'd like to discover its origin." I said, assembling my veggie patty. "I have a friend who works at a radiocarbon and sourcing lab. I'll give her a sample to test. Until then I'm limited to internet research." I took a nibble, continuing. "I've been researching voodoo a bit more. A voodoo statue can be very powerful and either virtuous or evil, depending upon the spirit inhabiting it."

He smiled, exposing small but nearly perfect teeth. "So you carry it around with you knowing it may transmit malevolent power?"

"I just leave it on the boat." I lied. "It's possible power comes from the creator's faith and conviction. So if I don't believe, then it can't influence me."

He continued chewing his sandwich, taking petite bites in-between, listening intently.

"The Hopi, a Pueblo tribe, have kachina dolls representing good spirits for the most part. They represent their ancestors, plants, animals, human qualities and so forth. Most are benevolent, but they do have a demon kachina they use to frighten kids." I lit a cigarette, inhaling deeply. "The basic concept is the belief in a spirit residing in an object. The children are frightened because they truly believe its power."

"Haiti is not too far from the Bahamas, and they're known for practicing voodoo." He suggested before wandering off.

The sun sat low on the horizon, appearing golden and exceptionally large like a giant ball floating on the sea surface. Slowly it descended until it completely disappeared. Russ, Lucas and others drifted back to the picnic table. I tidied up the area and grabbed all the condiments.

"I'm taking these back to the boat." I said, lightly holding up the plastic bottles.

It appeared eerily dark in the cabin, with only a few dim lights from neighboring boats radiating a luminescent glow like a cluster of jellyfish in the deep blue sea. Not wanting to open the refrigerator, I grabbed a beer from the cooler, leaving the mustard and ketchup on the counter. I felt a presence, as if someone was watching me. I thought I heard breathing. A chill ran down my spine, and I quickly turned and left. I felt like I carried a glow stick as I found my way back to the group.

A slightly tipsy Russ winked at me. "So pescatarian, do you play the hook game or pool?"

Tilting my head, "I play pool and I've heard of Captain Hook.

Any relation?"

He cracked a smile, "Let's go play in the yacht club. I'll teach you."

Russ took the lead as a gaggle of dogs followed, including Yoda and a stray yellow lab. Lucas and his buddies lingered at the bar, passing cocktails from the bartender. Russ and I walked across to the game room.

Russ held a silver circle in his hand attached to plastic fishing line. The object of the game was to throw the circle onto a hook attached to the wall. He tossed the swinging line ten times, hooking two. He handed me the dangling circle the size of a golf ball. I flung it too aggressively and it bounced off the wall three times.

"Easy," he said. "Like your hitching a tame horse, not a mustang."

I giggled at his lingo, but understanding the gist I threw more gently, only bouncing the hook off the wall once. It still swung wildly, but somewhat closer to the target. I played with my footing and focused on the task at hand, finally getting the circle to catch within ten throws. I threw my hands in the air and jumped up and down. "Yeah."

"Much better," he said. "A rematch?"

"Hell yeah. I got the hang of it now."

He rolled his eyes, and started the challenge. He managed three hooks in his ten shots. He grinned assuming a win, and then handed me the ring. "Your turn."

I studied the angles and found my best swing. Concentrating on the target, I hit the hook on my first throw, and then the third. I missed four and five but hit six, seven and nine. I felt like Duane Wade on his best night. I waved my hands in the air, turning towards Russ. "Told you I had this," I said adding, "Do you want a rematch or a pool tournament?"

"I think you may be a pool shark, but let's give it a try." he said.

I noticed Jeff and Jenny walk into the bar, I swayed to the upbeat Bahamian music and accidentally pocketed the eight ball, forfeiting the game.

Jeff approached, "Can I play this one against Raves?" He asked Russ, his words slightly slurred.

"Sure." Russ stepped aside.

I racketed the balls and started the game with the break and no balls went into the side pocket.

Jeff pocketed a stripe and then said in a raspy whisper, "Where's the idol Raves?"

He took me off guard. "What? I showed you my idol."

"Where is it now Raves?"

"Why? It's just a statue. Nothing more." My stomach uncontrollably flip-flopped as I backed away from him. "I think you've had too much to drink."

He stepped closer, whispering through his small teeth, his icy blue eyes turning dark grey. "I felt its heat through the hole on its head."

"It looks nothing like the one you're searching for." I shot back. "Jenny showed me her drawing."

"Ha. She's got a great imagination." He scowled and grabbed my wrist. "Where is it?"

"Let go of her." Russ said sternly. He now stood next to me, glowering at Jeff.

I pulled away from his grip. "He's had too much to drink."

"What's going on? Raves are you okay?" Lucas asked, appearing with Jenny next to him.

"Yes I'm fine, just a bit shaken up. Let's get a few drinks and go back to the bungalow, I'll explain there." I looked at Jenny. "I think your husband needs some rest. He's not making sense."

A few drinks and moments later, the two of us sat on the balcony overlooking the clear gentle surf, under an abundance of stars. My cigarette seemed to taste better, perhaps because of the briny air.

"So what happened with Jeff?" he asked.

"He asked the location of my idol over and over and then got hostile. He thinks it's the same one he's been seeking. I don't care how drunk he was, he's creepy. Earlier, while putting away condiments on the big boat, I sensed someone watching me and I could have sworn I heard breathing. I think he may have been in there. It was so dark, I just turned around and left. Good thing my idol isn't on the boat."

"He better not touch you again or I'll break his arm. Perhaps he's just a bad drunk. But you don't grab or push any woman, period."

"We leave tomorrow, so I don't think it will happen again. Earlier in the day, he seemed cordial over small talk. We discussed voodoo and he seemed more knowledgeable than most about the subject. He even suggested I consider Haiti as the origin of the statue since it's so close.

"No, we're not going to Haiti. First Cuba and now Haiti?"

"I didn't say let's go to Haiti. But since you mention it." I wickedly smiled, knowing it would be the last place he'd want to visit. "Just saying."

I dreamt I was in Africa dancing and spinning wildly to pounding drums in an arena full of spectators. The crowd screamed, cheered and upon closer inspection, I realized they were all cloth voodoo dolls with needles protruding from different parts of their pliable bodies. In the center of the crowd sat a gigantic pink tinted stele bearing a clear inscription, *Nothing further beyond.*

CHAPTER ELEVEN

JUNE 1, 2011

STANIEL CAY TO NASSAU

"Good Morning," I called up to Russ, who stood confidently on the bridge. He was barefoot, wearing only navy swim trunks and a baseball cap with a colorful Guy Harvey sailfish design. His chest and belly were pale and a bit doughier than I had imaged. He no longer looked like a cowboy, but the first impression he'd made as one would always be imprinted in my mind.

He smiled widely, turning towards me. "It's always a good morning in the Bahamas. Is Lucas ready?"

Throwing my bags on the stern, I answered. "He's right behind me, he just had to settle the bill and grab some coffee." At 7:00 am, the dock seemed marginally busy with a few fishermen prepping for the day, while others had already departed. Noticing *Davy Jones, Hillbilly Express,* and other familiar boats dark and quiet, I imagined the owners were sleeping off their hangovers, especially Jeff. I had no desire to see him ever again. Russ agreed to take the smaller room, so I arranged our belongings in the master bedroom where the Kramers previously slept.

I joined Russ on the bridge where he conversed with my honey standing on the dock.

"I'm ready to move out with the Intrepid," Lucas announced. "We'll tie up about five miles out.

He released our lines and we were off for New Providence

Island and the Bahamian capital, Nassau. The waters were calm as we floated past *Thunderball* Grotto. I wanted to explore more of the outer islands, but realized the danger posed by the faulty *Cabin Fever* and possible looming hurricane. We were supposed to cross over to Cat Island with the Kramers after Staniel, but all the complications annihilated our original plan. I was looking forward to Cat, supposed location of some of the best fishing in the Bahamas. I imagined us eventually vacationing there.

"Any news on the tropical storm?" I asked, sitting on the cushion next to Russ.

"Yes. It's named Athena and heading in our general direction," he answered. "It won't be a problem today, but we need to keep a close eye on it."

"So, what's the difference between a tropical storm and a hurricane? I know a hurricane is stronger, what wind speed differentiates the two?"

He glanced at me with a wink and a smile, "While on the water, they are both dangerous. A cat one starts at 74 mph. You've really never been in a hurricane?"

"No, just tornados and earthquakes." I said. "A few earthquakes in southern California and a tornado while working in Texas."

"Ah, so you're not from Florida I take it?"

"No, I just live there now. I grew up in Las Vegas and San Pedro, just outside Los Angeles."

"City girl."

I snickered, "More like world earth-loving girl. And south Florida isn't exactly country. Miami is quite large, bigger than Vegas."

His smile grew wider, as he casually ran his fingers through his ample hair. "I grew up in Everglades City, due west of Miami, but not quite as far as Naples. I reside in Jupiter now, and both are far from Miami in size and population. Besides, I'm just messing with you pescatarian. I like the city."

I grinned back. "And I like the country. And city and ocean and the exotic and --"

He interrupted me. "Okay, I get it."

"I've never been to Everglades City. I've seen it on the map, it seems a bit out there. Surrounded by swamp I suppose."

"As country as you could imagine. Population is less than a

thousand, even back in its drug smuggling hay day. It's gator country, with hundreds of small islands, known as Ten Thousand Islands. A hell of a place to grow up. Lots of fun on air boats, fishing and hunting. You'd like it. We have the best seafood in Florida."

I grinned at the thought of scooting around in an airboat for transportation, perhaps wrestling a gator while chasing off drug thugs. "They had drug running in the Everglades?"

"Hell almost the entire town was involved, profiting from the marijuana trade. Including my family. Brothers and cousins, not me," he insisted. "Runners would drop bags from the air and they'd pick them up by boat. From there it was an easy run, until Reagan waged his war on the drug trade during the 80's. All the better, I guess."

He pointed to *Breakfast in Bimini* slowing down in front of us. "Can you take the helm? I need to help with the lines."

"Yes captain."

"Just keep the boat centered on a heading of 330."

"Yes sir," I mumbled as I scooted into the captain's chair.

I watched the two toss around lines and then Lucas dove into the shallow water, emerging on the stern. Looking up at me, he shouted, "I think Raves is a captain now, so we can go relax."

They giggled like school boys. I concentrated on maintaining my heading. *I can do this,* I told myself. *It's easier than piloting since I didn't have to watch my altitude. The boat also seemed steadier than the Intrepid.*

The ocean looked peaceful as we passed the Exuma island chain on the starboard. No boats were visible in the immediate vicinity. Ripples in the sea hinted at a slight wind. A splash in the distance suggested a larger fish, perhaps a dolphin or wahoo had surfaced. I still wasn't sure what fish were likely at different times in particular locations and depths, a knowledge experienced fishermen held like a shaman protecting his magical potions and cures. The two men surfaced near the helm.

"I thought you two were going to relax." I felt like they were pushing me out of my captain duties.

"Yeah, no." Lucas answered, bumping me from the chair. "You can rest, read or something."

"Fine, I'll do yoga on the bridge." The two looked at me blankly.

I already had on my workout clothes out of habit, not knowing what else to wear when I awakened. I used a towel as my mat and started my yoga flow. The slight sway of the boat didn't affect my poses, in fact my body seemed to mindlessly adjust my balance and concentration. I performed a few floor stretches breathing in the fresh unfiltered saline and slightly fishy air. I breathed deeper, inhaling nature. The guys were tuned into their own navigation program, not giving any attention to my workout. I did my final pose, the resting pose, *Savasana*. I concentrated on the sounds around me with my eyes closed. I imagined a third eye in-between my eyebrows to clear my mind and focus. I heard the slight sound of our inboard motors, soothing waves lapping, a few seagull caws, and then a raspy whisper came, "Return me."

I shuddered into consciousness, bolting up with a dismissive yet silent, "What? Fuck off demon." I felt giddy, yet confident it was only my mind playing tricks on me. I had to investigate the idol more, because returning it to the sea wouldn't reveal the mysterious secrets it held. It chose me and I was the right person to find its origins.

I gave Uga-Bugga the evil eye on my way to the sparsely lit shower. One small window provided enough natural glow for a brief soap-up and rinse. For the remainder of the cruise we had no electric, so I flushed the toilet with a few up and down hand pumps. I slid into my island attire, a yellow and white bikini with matching wrap. Grabbing the idol, I placed it in my duffle bag so I didn't have to look at it. "Punishment," I whispered, walking away after picking up my book.

Back on the bridge with the guys I settled into a sun drenched lounge chair to continue reading, *Turning the Tide*. The sun was now hostile and unforgiving. The air felt thick with humidity, the slight breeze of our eight-knot speed providing little relief. Within a half-hour my already tanned skin turned sepia.

I took shelter from the powerful rays by joining Russ at the shaded helm. Country music played softly through the speakers, and Lucas had disappeared into the cabin prior to my arrival. "So you're fine just navigating with the compass?" I asked, leaning back almost horizontal with my feet propped up. "I mean, isn't it better to have the GPS and depth finder?"

He swung his captain's chair towards me and smiled. "A compass is all we really need. Are the other instruments useful?

Yes, but I've been boating all my life before the GPS was even invented. Our depth is shallow today."

"Funny, you don't look that old," I said. "Did you use a sextant too?"

"Honey, I'm by no means old. Just been all around these islands, a few times and back."

"So what's your favorite?"

"Oh, tough question." He paused with reflection. "I like Cat Island and Rum Cay." He paused again, "And this funny town off the northern tip of Eleuthera called Spanish Wells." His grinned widened.

I smiled with him and asked, "Why is it funny?"

"To start with, most of the island is populated with white Bahamians known as loyalists. The lobster industry thrives there, and teenagers circle the island on golf carts, cruising around like many American teens. It's a dry town. No alcohol is sold on the island."

I giggled. "It doesn't sound like fun."

He glanced at me, "Oh, but it is. I didn't know this the first time I went, so when I ran out of rum and asked around for a liquor store, I found out the nearest one was on a neighboring island. And I would have to take the ferry, but the liquor store closed five minutes ago."

"No," I breathed.

He nodded. "But, this stranger knew where to get liquor on the island, from a man named Buddha.

"Buddha sells beer?" I teased.

"Oh, he sells more than beer. So I jump into this stranger's car and within a few minutes I'm knocking on Buddha's door. He takes me out back to his private liquor store. Hundreds of liquor bottles, cases upon cases of beer, cigarettes and hash if I wanted it."

"Buddha does hash too?"

He shot me a sideways look. "Anyway, I got a bottle of rum and some beer from a large rotund Bahamian named Buddha."

I laughed, and called to Lucas when I saw him approaching, "Honey, did you know Buddha does hash and smuggles alcohol?"

He looked at me as if I had a third eye. "Okay." He handed me a PB&J sandwich and Russ a ham, turkey and cheese. Three beers accompanied our lunch.

Ignoring my comment, he told us of his morning emails and his thoughts about the storm and boat situation. His fervor for weather and the elements of nature embodied his whole being. It seemed almost excessive at times, to the point of being obsessive-compulsive, but a great trait to have for a boat captain and pilot.

"So I arranged for our plane to be in Bimini tomorrow," Lucas unemotionally announced. "Gary…" He glanced towards Russ clarifying, "Our past instructor, is dropping off my Cessna in Bimini and then returning on a commercial flight. He's flying over a boat captain, leaving our plane while the captain paid for his return flight." He took a swig from his bottle. "It's a win-win situation."

So we have two boats and a plane. Seems like overkill, I thought but didn't say.

"Well, it's good to have a backup. But probably not necessary." Russ said.

"I know, but I'd rather have a plan in place in case Athena gets out of hand. The last place I'd want to be during a hurricane is Bimini, and the projected track and conditions are not looking good."

I shuddered, realizing for the first time the name of the storm and then tilted my head towards the two. "Do they usually name hurricanes after Greek gods?"

"Recently, they are trying to be politically correct and use a variety of ethnic names." Lucas answered. "With the strange names people are naming their kids nowadays, it's not unusual."

"Well she is the goddess of Athens and she defeated Poseidon, the god of the sea, for the title."

The two looked at me blankly.

"Just saying."

"So you like those foreign gods and idols?" Russ asked with a Cheshire cat grin. "I didn't have a chance to look at your idol, can I see it?"

"Sure cowboy," I answered, and then ran down the stairs to retrieve the effigy from my bag. Holding the idol in my hand, I narrowed my eyes, squinting and whispering, "Be good and stop haunting me." I felt unreasonably suspicious of the artifact, and quickly corrected my thoughts. After all, I was a scientist, not a psychic. I knew the mind could be cunning, overpowering rationality.

Thoughts of Jamie's words about 'the mind being a tricky thing' shifted my thoughts towards her and their fiery oil disaster. I wondered how they were making out. I'd hoped the media storm would fizzle out with new and exciting stories to cover, but that didn't seem likely unless something else major happened soon. Perhaps a hurricane would divert the mass media's attention.

Reentering the bridge, I listened to Lucas retell the hurdles we encountered in the past week as if they were a comedy-drama film he recently watched. He emphasized the look on my face when Kevin from Norman's told me the duck came through a portal. They cackled as I placed the idol in Russ' hand.

"It's a beauty, isn't it?" I gloated.

He raised his eyebrows, examining the artifact from the captain's chair. "It's different. What's the hole in its head for?"

I shrugged. "I don't know. It's part of the mystery. I need to research it more when I have access to faster internet. A library and some archaeological colleagues will certainly help. Being at sea without my connections, I can only guess."

Searching the console and radio box, he pulled out a tiny LED flashlight from the compartment, promptly sticking it into the crown cavity. He studied it, shifting angles of the statue and flashlight as if preparing to extract a tooth. Reaching for his pocket knife, he jammed it into the gap, fussed around, and then turned it upside down while shaking it vigorously. A small crystal rolled into his hand.

My eyes widened, "Holy crap."

"It just might be," he kidded.

I plucked the small crystal from his hand. Holding it up to the sun rays I noticed it had a clear rose tint and six distinct sides, a perfect hexagon. Its reflection from the sun sent me into a momentary trance as the amplified radiance mesmerized me. I felt like I was one with of the universe, and for a brief moment, time stood still. I searched my mind for similar crystals from my collection as an amateur rock-hound. Nothing I possessed radiated perfection like the quartz sparkling in my palm. In fact, nothing I'd experienced before held its energy. My body heat rose resembling a hot-flash, something I'd never felt but understood. I sensed the two men gawking at me.

"Wow," I stuttered.

"Well, what is it?" Lucas asked impatiently.

I blinked back to reality and joked, "I don't know but it just gave me an orgasm." The two stared at me. "Just kidding." I pushed the gemstone towards them, "It's a quartz crystal. A perfect, beautiful one."

"What does it mean, and why is it stuffed into a wooden statue?" Russ asked.

"I don't know." I wondered. "But it's certainly not an accident. My need to research and its magnitude has just multiplied. And this means Jeff was right. He's been searching for a crystal idol or more precisely, a powerful crystal inside an ancient idol." My heart fluttered. I recalled my internet search, "This crazy website I found said certain crystals are programmed for finding portals." I laughed at myself. "If it vibrates and warms immensely, then a portal is close-by." It definitely warms, I thought.

Lucas's eyes widened. "Honey, what kind of other stuff are you messing with?"

I breathed a concerned snicker. "I have to think about this. An ice cold beer would really help."

"Well, check into the Bimini Road and the lost city of Atlantis during your investigation." Russ said, emphasizing "investigation" as if it suddenly had a profound new meaning. Considering you found it on the beach there." His amber eyes held my gaze longer than necessary. He seemed to sense my uneasiness, quickly breaking eye contact and scanning the sea.

"I don't believe in lost cities," I said, stuffing the crystal back into the effigy's cavity, aggressively pushing it back down with the pocket knife. I knew my comment wasn't completely true. Cities get abandoned and rediscovered throughout history, like the Mayan temples rediscovered in the jungles of Mexico and Guatemala just in the past century. The Incas Machu Picchu relocated by Hiram Bingham. Heinrich Schliemann's locating and excavation of the legendary city of Troy. Many, many more lay in all parts of the world, some yet to be discovered. But Atlantis in the new world? I wasn't yet convinced. This idol undoubtedly held a mystery, an anomaly whose challenge I welcomed.

He winked and smiled in my direction, "Why not? I don't know much about it except new age travelers visit Bimini in droves for the mystery and…what do they call it, energy or vortexes? I've seen them on the island on a pilgrimage, or something similar."

I scanned the bridge for Lucas, who had vanished, silently

hoping he would return with several beers. I needed a drink to calm me, and a Kalik light seemed like the perfect choice.

"You don't seem like the type who would believe in new age pilgrimages," I teased.

"You've got that right, but I do pay attention to what's going on around me. After all, I've been visiting Bimini on a regular basis for over twenty years. I see trends on the island come and go. Now it's popular to visit the Bimini Road and some sort of vortex, from what I've heard tourists talk about."

I recalled my mom mentioning Sedona vortexes as part of her spiritual quest. A multiple dimension of healing energy she experienced among the red rocks. I'd figured she took some mind enhancing drug like Peyote or Jimson Weed, commonly used by Native Americans. But magical otherworldly energy prompting people to visit Bimini?

Smiling at the thought of Russ discussing a vortex and new agers, I sat on a port-side cushion, placing the idol next to me. He seemed so far from a believer in anything remotely metaphysical or spiritual. Perhaps that had been a faulty initial judgment, since I really didn't know him well, but I wanted to learn more about this cowboy with piercing, golden-brown eyes.

I felt a favonian breeze bristle my arm hair, cooling me slightly. "So do you normally boat alone or with family and friends?" I asked.

"A little of both. Whoever wants to come along." He glanced at his heading then back at me. "I was married for eighteen years. My wife and son loved the water as much as I do. My son still boats with me when he's not busy with college and girls. He lives in Gainesville with some college buddies, but I'm perfectly at home solo on the water."

Being childless, I didn't understand. I imagined if I didn't have a miscarriage, my child would be applying for college about now, or at least soon. I tried not to think about his or her age and what might have been.

Looking past Russ, I spotted a sailboat in the distance, the first boat I'd seen since we left Staniel. It rocked gently like an empty hammock in a light breeze under a cloudless sky. I had been periodically scanning the horizon since discovering the crystal, consciously looking for the *Davy Jones* boat. Past the sailboat, pale blue water and white sand hinted at a petite deserted island. A larger one loomed to the north, only distinguishable as a shadow with matchsticks I recognized as trees.

"And the wife?"

"Ex-wife," he corrected. "We just grew apart. She wanted another child and I didn't. Nothing dramatic, I just couldn't stand the bickering. We're still friends. I'm even friends with her new husband." He grinned. "I just wanted to go to sea and live a peaceful life, not start over with a newborn when I already had a son in high school."

I nodded. "Understandable. So did she have another kid?"

"Not yet, and she probably won't, but she has two dogs and a cat. I've never liked pets, another thing we'd bicker about."

I laughed. "Unheard of. How can you not like cute fuzzy creatures? I imagine they're easier than kids."

He snickered. "How can you not eat steak and burgers? Personal preference."

He was right.

"Do you own fuzzy beasts or have kids?" he asked.

"Just my cat, Karma. A coworker is watching her while I'm gone. Between working long hours at the museum and spending most nights with Lucas, I can't really have more than a low maintenance kitty. Karma is pretty laid back and takes care of herself." I paused for a moment, watching a pelican dive-bomb into the sea. "I have a few carefree weeks off with no responsibilities. Too bad we have to head back to Florida."

"Well, the boat and the weather aren't cooperating. During a tropical storm or hurricane you just don't want to be on the water. This ship is a floating time-bomb."

Lucas appeared again, restocking the cooler with a case of beer, handing us a few cold ones. He took over captain duties, changing the music from country to reggae. Russ vanished into the cabin, resurfacing on a sun-drenched lounge chair. His pale skin in the light resembled the enamel of his bright smile.

I reclined across from Lucas with my book in hand and idol by my head. I read a few chapters, took a few cigarette breaks on the stern, studied the idol a few times and made sure Lucas, Russ and I always had a cold Kalik. The ocean was unchanging, calm and serene. An occasional fish jumped, reminding me I was still at sea. I didn't observe a single vessel after the last sailboat we spotted, the indistinct islands still lingering in the background.

"What islands are those?" I asked above the music.

"They're all part of the Exumas, hundreds of small islands with the largest in the chain being Great Exuma, just south of Staniel." He scanned the horizon and pointed east, "Over in that direction, is Eleuthera. Right now we're not far from Norman's, although it's hard to tell without GPS." His gaze shifted to me. "But I know about where we are…based on time, and the paper map if we need it. Allen's Cay will be the last island prior to crossing toward Nassau, then heading back through the Yellow Bank."

"Oh, not the Yellow Bank." I hesitated and asked, "Are we looking for corals again?"

He smiled confidently. "We have perfect weather conditions today. Flat calm with good visibility. Not a cloud in the sky and if a rainstorm popped up, I'd be eerily surprised. We can see everything from the bridge."

"Oh, watch what you say. Now you're challenging Uga-Bugga. And I'm not sure you want to, since we messed with the crystal lodged in his skull."

He shot me a sideways look. "It's probably a she, unpredictable as it is."

"Hey, I resemble that remark," I teased.

"After we clear the Yellow Bank, we can hop into the Intrepid and troll pre-dusk when the fish are more active."

"Are you trying to seduce me on a deserted island again?" I asked, blowing him an air kiss and a wink. I glanced back at Russ napping in the sun and then back to my sweetie. "He's sleeping. We could just get it on right here."

He chuckled. "Yes honey, great idea."

Approaching the Yellow Bank, I noticed a few cumulus clouds popping up. There wasn't a cloud in the sky all day until now, and they were quickly rising.

"Those look like tropical storm clouds. I hope they're not forming over us." Luke said anxiously.

"Do you want me on the bow looking for coral?" I asked.

"Yes, please." A cloud covered the sun, obstructing the clarity of water depth and color. My polarized glasses provided better visibility.

"Russ, I need your help spotting corals."

I noticed a large darker area. We have one at our 12:00," I called out.

Our course shifted ten degrees right. "Will this heading keep us clear?" Lucas asked.

"Yes." Russ appeared by my side and then went to the opposite railing.

"After you clear I need ten degrees left," Russ said.

The boat shifted again. "I have something, but I'm not sure if it's an issue."

Russ came to my side momentarily, examining our location relative to the coral. "You're fine on this heading," He called out, quickly returning to starboard.

The sky turned slightly darker as a thicker cloud covered the sun. I could still read the water, but it became more difficult to distinguish the spots farther out. I didn't see any menacing storms, or hear any thunder.

"Ten left." Russ called out, followed by an urgent "Make it twenty, now!"

The boat turned sharply, and I wondered how we stayed on course, deviating without a GPS. I saw a large protruding coral, and after passing we shifted back to the right. It seemed like we were encountering more coral heads than last time.

The clouds cleared the sun, allowing better visibility. They were still in the area, billowing thousands of feet into the sky. They looked like cauliflower clusters stacked on top of one another. I noticed a bulky object in the distance.

After a while we returned to the helm where we monitored the seas for the diminishing corals. "A perfect sky all day, until we hit the Yellow Bank." Russ said. "Go figure. The tropical storm must be moving faster than predicted."

"Unless another one is forming in this area." Lucas said. "It has happened."

The object came into clearer view as we traversed closer. I finally pointed off the bow. "Do you guys see that ship? Straight ahead, it looks like a freighter or something."

Lucas squinted and picked up the binoculars. He stared through them, adjusting the focus. "What the hell. It looks like an old steamer." He handed the optical device to Russ. "What do you make of it?"

Russ studied the ship, his lips forming an uncertain expression. "It certainly looks like a steamer." He ran his fingers though his hair. "I've never seen one in these waters. We have to check it out." Russ pushed the throttle forward and passed the Bushnell's to me. "Any thoughts Raves?"

I immediately noticed its weathered appearance, rusty and battered, something I'd expect to excavate not see floating at sea. The only steam engines I've seen were riverboats used for sightseeing. They usually had a large paddlewheel propelling them from behind. This one lacked the bulky wheel, but a rusty circular stack sat near its rear. It seemed to be moving slowly. I scanned the deck for its crew and spotted none. My stomach fluttered with uncertainty, and I couldn't tell if it was from excitement or fear.

"Let's get closer to see what we can find out." I said.

I held Lucas's concerned gaze for a moment as we approached. Still no crew appeared. The long steamer cruised steadily at about 3 knots. We checked out the stern and then the port side. The name on the side of the ship read *Cotopaxi*. I glanced at Russ, who appeared pale. "What's wrong?" I asked.

"Nobody's at the helm. I haven't seen a single person on this ship." He said in an irritated tone. "How is that possible?"

"Something obviously happened to the crew." Lucas said.

"Is there a way to climb aboard?" I asked.

"Yes, from the stern." He looked at me. "It's too dangerous."

"Come on. If we can safely board, we can figure out what's going on." I paused. "And if not, then at least we're not left wondering if we should have."

"Russ can you maneuver and idle near the stern for a few minutes? We'll be brief."

Our bow aligned with the *Cotopaxi*'s stern and Lucas grabbed the ladder. "Go ahead, I'm right behind you."

"This ship is huge. Let's go to the bridge." I said, once I reached the deck, moving quickly to the middle of the freighter. We passed the engine room and glanced inside. This is eerie. What happened to the crew? No bodies, nothing."

"The engine looks intact," he said.

"I'd like to find the captain's quarters." I kept moving forward and peeked into the next room. "The helm." I announced.

"Wheelhouse," Lucas corrected.

I quickly searched for anything. A rusty plaque caught my eye. *Clinchfield Navigation Company 1918.* "Holy crap. This ship is from 1918." My thoughts raced. Why is it here, intact but vacant? I opened empty cabinets.

"Keep moving Raves. Check out one more room, and then we have to go."

"We have a stateroom," I announced, opening drawers. "And I found a revolver and diary."

"Grab them and let's go. I'm not comfortable here. Something's wrong with this ship."

Russ picked us up from the stern, "So what did you find?"

"It's a ghost ship, but I found some notes and a gun." I exhaled a long breath. "It's pretty creepy."

I opened the captain's log to a few scribbled journal entries, the last record caught my eye and I read it aloud. *1 December 1925. The compass is spinning out of control. The ship is being pulled towards a green light. Attempts to maneuver away from the mysterious glow failed. Something else is in control of this vessel.*

The three of us silently looked at each other with alarm.

We watched the orange disc of the sun fade into the ocean, arriving in the marina as a fuchsia glow sparkled and danced on the horizon. We didn't land at the lavish Atlantis marina, but a more subdued harbor on cable beach called Sandyport. It was a quiet harbor compared to Staniel, but welcome.

CHAPTER TWELVE

JUNE 2, 2011

NASSAU TO BIMINI, 2011

Smoke filled my lungs in what appeared to be the middle of the night, and for a fleeting moment I thought I was dreaming. I shook Lucas, simultaneously pushing out the screen and yelling, "Fire." In an instant impromptu swoosh I bolted through the screened-in window, effortlessly landing on the wooden dock. I unplugged the boat power cord from the electrical box.

Returning to the cabin through the slider, I opened all doors and windows shouting, "Lucas, Russ!" A pungent smell of smoke permeated the air. It wasn't thick, but thin and acrid, leaving a burning sensation in my eyes, and lungs.

The two emerged through the haze sporting only boxers. Lucas wore blue and white horizontal stripes, and Russ wore hunting camouflage. I remembered for the first time that I wore boxers, borrowed from my honey, and a loose tank top. I felt relieved to have on any clothing at all. We all stepped onto the dock for a breath of fresh air.

"Well, that's a helluva way to wake up," Russ exhaled. "It's not a fire, Raves. Fire means flames. It's smoke."

I blinked. Smoke usually meant fire, besides it was an instinctive reaction.

"Okay, my bad. I'm glad you unplugged the power." He looked around, "Why is the window screen on the dock?"

"Oh, welcome to my world," Lucas chimed in. "Raven screamed, "fire" in my ear, shook me into consciousness, then jumped through the screen and onto the dock."

Russ stared at me in disbelief. I answered before he could make any wry comments.

"Well, I had to do something, and I didn't know what was happening. My adrenaline just took over. So are things still sizzling inside? Has anyone checked yet?"

"You did the right thing by cutting off the power supply, it's like clipping the fuel supply to an engine. Let's go find out," Russ urged.

I stayed on the dock, admiring the sunrise for a moment as it painted the sky a pinkish orange, a phenomenon I didn't witness often, at least not lately. The stillness and tranquility of dawn amazed me, the vast calm sea only enhancing the serene moment. Waking up docked in the Bahamas was an experience unlike any other, the way life should be lived. Natural sounds of waves tenderly hitting the dock pilings, fresh slightly saline air, made me feel peaceful and carefree. In the distance, dozens of seagulls lined up along a pool's edge, dipping their coal beaks and small avian bodies. Boisterously calling each other, several broke off for a quick flight, causing a domino effect resembling planes after flying in formation, each bird cutting off in different directions, spaced only seconds apart. They'd come back to the pool's edge displacing other seagulls, and the scene repeated itself.

I craved coffee, but without power or any nearby businesses I'd have to skip it. I ducked back on board, and changed into my running clothes. "I have time to run, right?" I asked, scooting past Lucas.

"Yes, honey. We have to check the wires and weather again before setting sail." He glanced at me, adding, "And reinstall the window screen."

I snickered, knowing I had done the right thing.

My jog took me through the marina, to some quaint ocean side homes and a few resorts along a vacant road, devoid of any sign of life. I found myself amazed by the lack of activity on this side of the island. We were on Bahamas time, generally with no real urgency for anything. I blissfully listened to my audiobook, and the description of a daunting adventure at sea. I giggled at our unnerving ocean journey, a bit relieved I didn't have to deal with a tiger and orangutan on board the Bluewater, despite our strange encounters and technical issues. I just hoped hurricane Athena and the boat wiring would be okay for our final two legs of the trip.

After forty-five minutes I ended up back at the marina, snatching a water bottle and asking nonchalantly, "So, what's the news?"

"The hurricane has strengthened, and we're in the cone of death. The rubber hoses in the thru-hull are burned, the toilets and air conditioning are not working, and Gary dropped off your plane in Bimini," Russ matter-of-factly answered.

My eyes widened as I drank my water. "Cone of death?"

"It's the predicted path of Athena, right through Bimini to Fort Lauderdale."

"I told you guys Athena has made Poseidon angry. But nobody listens." I teased.

Russ shot me a sideways look. "I'm not sure if that's true. In fact, I know it's not, but we are setting sail in twenty minutes, so go to the marina and shower and do what you need to do. Lucas is there now."

"Okay cowboy." A large smile graced my face. I meandered to the amenities with my towel, toiletries, and bathing suit in hand, unintentionally humming the song "Breakfast at Tiffney's." I felt well-balanced and at one with nature, almost euphoric as I silently giggled at my jump through the screen at dawn. I appreciated the marine lifestyle more, although not yet second nature for me as it seemed for other seafarers I'd encountered over the past week. I'd get comfortable enough someday.

Arriving back at the dock, I found the men ready to go with the two boats already hitched and the engine running on the *Cabin Fever*. I helped Lucas untie the lines and we joined Russ on the bridge. The ocean held only a slight ripple as if an angel breathed a tender divine puff of wind.

A dreamy calm before the storm, I thought. I recalled our experience just days prior with the pitch and roll of the boat, and waves crashing over the stern. I knew the sea could be erratic and as unpredictable as an earthquake, a far cry from the tranquility currently surrounding us.

"So what's the accuracy of the predicted cone of death?" I asked.

Lucas and Russ looked at each other sagely, and Lucas

responded, "Well, this far out the cone is pretty wide, and it can change daily. Right now they have us in the center, so we'll probably feel its effects no matter which way it shifts. Unless they're completely blowing the forecast, which is also possible." He backed away from the controls and sat next to me, leaving Russ at the wheel. Placing his hand on my knee, he said "You'll get your first hurricane even if we're not in the center, or at least your first tropical storm."

"I think the eye will go right over Bimini," Russ announced without trepidation. "But by then we'll be back in Florida, putting up hurricane shutters."

"And having hurricane parties." Lucas joked.

My eyes widened. "Don't we have to stock up on food, water and prepare for a disaster? It's what all the news channels encourage, but you guys don't seem concerned."

"We have enough food on this boat to last months," Russ drawled.

Lucas warmly looked into my eyes. "Only, if its intensity is greater than a category three. It's too early to tell. We'll know more tonight and tomorrow. And we have a generator back home, so if we lose power we'll be fine."

"I know I'm fine with you, my Hercules." I replied. "It sounds better than an earthquake. Those things scare the hell out of me.

"Oh, it's nothing to take lightly if it's a cat four or five." Lucas said. "Andrew, a small but strong category five, decimated parts of Miami. I went to help clear debris from neighborhoods. It was devastating for those in the eye."

"I took my truck and helped too," said Russ. "I saw boats on top of houses, and trees. It looked unrecognizable."

A few small bare-minimum Bahamian boats sped by, not as a group but independently. They all looked similar, with only slight variations. They were weathered grey, had the smallest possible single outboard, were topless with no shade to escape the sun's radiation, and had a single bench with controls close enough to the rear to hand control the engine if needed. One or two men manned each. I imagined them going out for the day's catch. Perhaps conch, lobster, grouper or barracuda.

The marina and eventually the entire island slowly disappeared from view. I thought about the Atlantis allegory, vortexes, and supernatural beliefs among the Native Americas, West Africans,

Mayans, and Incans. They were all ancient practices I was somewhat familiar with, but not an expert in. The pink crystal shoved in the idol's skull mystified me, but the captain's log and an empty ship from 1925 could only be explained as supernatural.

"Should we report the ship we saw yesterday to anybody?" I asked.

"What are we going to do? Call coast guard and tell them we saw a steamer from the 1920's, cruising empty?" Russ said. "They'd have us all committed, or simply not believe us."

"Maybe others have come across it. What do you two make of it? I know for me, it's opened my mind to the possibility of other dimensions and paranormal events."

Lucas blinked a few times. "I never thought I'd hear those words from your lips, but I feel the same way."

"Well, I consider us lucky to have seen it. The Bermuda Triangle revealed one of her mysteries." Russ said. "I just don't care to see it again, or anything else strange. Can you get me a beer Raves?"

I packed a small cooler with beer and water, and prepped a plate with cheese and crackers. Back on the bridge, I offered them both and then relaxed in the back with my book. My skin felt damp with perspiration from the intense sun. In the distance I heard the guys talking slightly above the country music and the lightness of lapping water. In every direction the ocean vastness dominated. I covered a few chapters of the history of drug smuggling in the Bahamas. I imagined what it would be like to live on Norman's Cay back then, as part of the Cartel with all the money flowing and armed guards patrolling beaches. A far cry from the tropical paradise surrounding us.

I heard Lucas shout, "Pilot whales."

I hurried to the helm. Medium size whales surrounded the boat as we slowed to a crawl, down to four knots. The view of the creatures from above was magnificent as they floated close to the surface.

"Want to jump in and see them underwater?" Lucas suggested.

"I'm good from here," I answered.

"Come 'on, sweetie."

"Go ahead," Russ urged. "I'll turn off the engine and the snorkel gear is on the stern."

I followed Lucas, fixing the mask and snorkel on my head and then jumping in. I couldn't see bottom at first, making me anxious. I slowly swam up to the face of one of the whales, its peaceful eye calming my fears, appearing tiny in its bulbous head. Another whale glided by, checking me out while my daring partner petted its fin. The whales were as black as a moonless night at sea. A few random scars appeared lighter, almost grey. I wondered what caused them, whether another creature or something man-made. I could hear a few faint deep whistles, them talking I imagined.

I felt Lucas firmly grab my hand, pulling me quickly through the water. His feet kicked frantically as did mine taking us both away from the whales. My heart raced not knowing why we hastily abandoned the scene. I wanted to return, finally comfortable in open water. Grabbing my ass with both hands, in one swoop he lifted me, pushing me onto the back of the boat as if I was a giant lobster he just speared.

"Get back," he bellowed, pulling himself onto the stern.

"What?" I asked, pulling off my gear. Wondering why we just didn't use the ladder.

"Whitetip shark," he panted. He slowed his breath and stood for a minute. "A whitetip was circling us, one of the most dangerous sharks in the Atlantic, and the first one I've ever encountered."

I stood speechless. I certainly didn't know much about sharks, but I knew Lucas wasn't afraid of most of them. I recalled whitetips as the first predators to appear at shipwrecks and plane crashes in the deep sea. Notorious for killing many of the survivors of the attack on the USS Indianapolis, one of the most gruesome shark encounters ever witnessed, the shark is considered by some to be more dangerous than the great white.

"Honey, give me a minute. My heart is racing."

We climbed to the top of the bridge, Lucas grabbed two beers and handed me one. Scanning the ocean, he pointed to the whales, positioning me to focus on where he was pointing. "Right there, you see its fin?"

I squinted without my sunglasses. "I think I see it near the undulations of the whales."

"I saw the fin follow you to the stern," Russ said. "It's the only time I saw it. By then I realized what's going on."

"A freaking whitetip. I thought they were only deep water sharks, or they just showed up at bloody accidents."

"I've heard they hang with Pilot whales, but I thought it was a myth." Russ threw out there.

Lucas's jaw dropped with an audible half laugh, half sigh. "You should have told me. I had no idea."

We picked up our pace, back to cruising speed. Famished, I made sandwiches for the three of us. While eating mine, I entertained myself by paging through National Geographic, ones I brought from my extensive collection.

Sitting in the shaded helm, I read short blurbs on new discoveries, technology and the environment. An article on Bowhead whales lured my interest, colossal in size compared to the smaller Pilot whales. I showed the guys scenic pictures, reading them facts from the article, but they didn't seem interested.

"It looks funny without a fin," Lucas commented.

They discussed fishing, placing a line in the water to see if they could get a bite, taking turns dangling it over the side rail below while the other managed the wheel.

"I'll take over as captain," I offered.

Lucas answered, "We got it."

I finished one magazine, and skimmed the next. A story on Santeria and its Afro-Cuban culture caught my eye. Originating in western Africa among the Yoruba people, it ended up in Cuba via the slave trade. Bringing their traditional religion with them, the slaves were forced to convert to Catholicism, incorporating their own spiritual beliefs into Christianity. Still practicing, they believed in one God, called Olodumare, communicating with the divine through rituals and divination. Statues acted as guides, the messenger of all gods known as St. Anthony or Eleggua. A picture on the page showed an elaborate statue of St. Anthony, so I compared it to my idol. I could see its African roots, but they were completely different. I perused the rest of the story for hints if my statue might be part of the practice.

After a while, Russ pointed out a speck barely visible on the horizon. "There's Bimini," he shouted.

Sitting up and squinting, I could make out a few vertical matchsticks in the distance. Trees, I guessed. I noticed a few flying fish soar above the sea from the corner of my right eye. The water looked marine blue with a gentle, barely noticeable swell. We hadn't seen another boat all day, and I found even the slight glimpse of land comforting.

"The boat's feeling pretty sluggish. Lucas can you check things out below?"

Five minutes later he returned with a disturbed grimace, addressing Russ, who stood adjacent. "We're taking on water. A lot." Raising his hand to his head, "I don't know if we can save this ship. I can't even find the source of the leak."

Silent tension hung in the air for a few seconds. Russ finally answered, "I'll check it out."

He slowed the engine to a crawl, "Raves take the wheel and keep us at a heading of 290. Lucas, let's go."

They disappeared into the belly of the ship as if entering the mouth of a whale. I paid close attention to my heading, occasionally looking back at the undulating Intrepid. It didn't move much in the diminutive wake of Bluewater, just a slight jiggle up and down with an occasional side step.

I scanned the smooth skyline and Bimini didn't seem any closer than the last time I checked. The matchsticks looked more robust, but no land had yet appeared. A light halo surrounded the island, a change in water color reflecting the shallower water and sand. I noticed for the first time an outline of a sailboat to the northwest, but I couldn't determine its direction or size. I heard the two men talking loudly down below and then heard a large splash. I spotted Lucas swimming toward the Intrepid. I was off course by five degrees, turning the wheel without much response from the compass. I remained slightly off my assigned heading as concern built in my mind. *Cabin Fever* seemed a bit lower in the water.

I watched Lucas climb aboard *Breakfast in Bimini*, untie her, start the engines and pull up next to us, idling at the starboard side of the Bluewater. Russ tossed several bags onto the smaller boat and then he ran up to the helm. "Raven..." He caught his breath for a moment, exhaling more calmly, "I put whatever bags you had packed onto the Intrepid. Check the cabin and grab everything you need, all your belongings and some food and drinks. We are sinking, but you have a little time."

My eyes widened, but after taking a few calming breaths. I replied, "Okay. What else can I do? Should I just grab everything, or just the necessities? Are you staying or coming with me?"

Standing erect and responding with equanimity, he intently repeated, "Collect any belongings we may have missed and some drinks, snacks and so forth from the galley. Hand them to Lucas.

You have five minutes. I'll stay on board until the last minute, when I know sinking's inevitable. Then I'll join you guys." He turned away and then shouted as I shot down the stairs with my magazine and sunscreen, "Grab the rum, please."

In the cabin, the water came up to my knees, sloshing around like a swimming pool in an earthquake. I checked the bedroom where everything was cleared. Next, I loaded a cooler and a few bags with water, beer, rum, wine, vodka, soda and non-perishables such as nuts, chips, peanut butter and jelly. I handed them over the side of the boat to Lucas and did a final check of the cabin, including the now empty dresser drawers. I filled one more bag with canned goods, bread, batteries, cups and some kitchen utensils.

Boarding the Intrepid, I immediately checked my luggage for my statue, running shoes and iPod. They were all mixed in with my bunched-up clothes. We idled in silence next to Russ, who still sat on the bridge, staring out to sea.

For a fleeting moment I wondered what the Kramers would say, and how Jamie would have handled the situation. Would she have gathered more supplies?

"Bimini's not far away," Lucas mournfully replied. "Just make sure you have what's personally important, because you won't see that ship again."

Shit the log book from the Cotopaxi, I hid it in a kitchen drawer. There was no way I was letting it go down with the ship.

"I forgot the captain's log," I said, jumping off the boat. I sloshed through the rising water, grabbed the log and hurried back to Lucas. "Got it." I stuffed it into my bag with the rest of my belongings.

I sighed a silent moan for the loss of an undependable boat. But a loss nonetheless. We'd had many trials and tribulations on board, but we also made new friends. The Kramers, Russ, Kate, Duff, maybe Jenny but certainly not Jeff. Characters like Oak and Larry stuck in my mind. I found myself connecting more deeply with Lucas over the course of just over a week. I came to understand and appreciate him, with a growing mutual bond, more than what I felt in months of dating, hanging out and having fun in Florida. In fact, even though we hadn't exchanged the words, "I love you," love was the only emotion to describe our deepened relationship. My heart warmed at the experiences we shared on the sinking boat.

Although I didn't lightly utter the powerful "L" word, I knew I would tell him at a more opportune time, just not while a boat under his command plummeted into the sea.

"Is Russ coming down soon...I mean is he okay?" I heard myself ask.

"I'm sure he'll be fine. He's just taking a moment. It's hard for a captain to see his ship go down." He gazed at me. "It just is. It's not technically his boat, but we both had a commitment to safely bring the Bluewater back to Florida."

I understood and respected the need for silence in this moment. I watched the water rise inside the boat, halfway up the glass sliders. Russ put on his cowboy hat, walked through them, and jumped onto *Breakfast in Bimini*.

"God damn piece of shit boat. Raves, can you pour me a rum and coke, please. A partial bag of ice is in the cooler you're sitting on."

I handed him a drink, and my sweetie a beer, opening one for myself as well. We cruised at a leisurely speed, silent except for the gentle sound of lapping waves.

Russ broke the silence. "I've never encountered a boat I couldn't fix. Mechanical, electrical, you name it, I can fix it. But not this disaster." He took a swig of his drink.

"So what happened down there?" I asked while watching the stern of *Cabin Fever* go under like the Titanic. The bow was sticking up at an angle, slowly following. Because of our personal experience, it seemed especially devastating. A complete loss of face for the captains, but thankfully no lives were lost. I felt empathy for the guys, including Nick, even though he didn't know yet.

"All the rubber thru-hulls completely burned and melted. It supplies the toilets, generator, engines, bilge pump, air-condition. I've never seen anything like it. The odds are just too great. And once it takes on that much water...forget it without a bilge."

"Well, the boat shouldn't have been in the rental pool. It gives the company a bad name and I'm going to tell them all about it. They should reimburse me for the trouble we endured, without the Intrepid we could have died out here. Who takes a charity boat with no history and rents it out?" Lucas retorted. "I'm sure they'll collect insurance money and do it again."

Not if it's an act of God, I pondered. It's even written into most insurance agreements. It clearly states if it's determined to be an act of God, then nothing is covered and all bets are off. Considering the bad juju my idol might carry, it could easily be classified as such. But more than likely they'd be covered under electrical problems. I looked back at the boat, barely visible above the water.

I refilled drinks all around and we picked up speed, Bimini bound. The island became more distinguishable, matchsticks maturing into palm trees with houses visible along the shore. The guys discussed going forward over the next few days. We would stay at Bimini Sands for two nights, recovering and relaxing a bit. From there Russ would run the Intrepid back to Florida and Lucas and I would fly his plane back to Fort Lauderdale. Of course our schedule and plans all depended upon the looming hurricane, Athena.

CHAPTER THIRTEEN

HAVANA, CUBA

JULY 1715

It had been just over a year ago that Akanni found the idol, on the same beach where she stood today. She felt its spiritual energy from the moment she touched its crown. It spoke to her, inspiring her to become an ordained priestess, a Santera. She chose Olokun as her spirit, consecrating her life to his service. It made complete sense to choose the ruler of the deep sea. The one who gathers sunken treasure and souls of the drowned. It had washed ashore just days after a French ship hit a reef during a hurricane. Although numerous men died, she believed Olokun saved just as many.

Akanni personalized her statue and made a shrine for her powerful saint. She fixed his burnt right leg, fashioning it into a bent knee with a cowrie shell to replace the missing foot. She glued cowrie shells into the eye sockets, and the perfectly circular hole in his right hand. She placed a veil made of blue lace over the cavity at the top of its head. Sometimes she noticed it radiating a greenish glow. Although it was her secret shrine, she allowed other priest and priestess visitation. Like her, they understood its healing power and contra wise, its ability to cause malevolence.

Akanni considered herself lucky as a domestic servant of a wealthy merchant. She managed the household, spending most of her day cleaning and rearing children. Although paid very little, she was able to return to her modest home every evening, unlike many slaves she knew who worked the fields.

The port bustled with hundreds of ships, with twelve of them preparing for a long voyage back to Spain. She noticed her friend loading barrels of tobacco aboard a large galleon. A hundred or so cannon lined the ship and it flew a yellow and red flag. Pens on the main deck held pigs, cattle, goats and chickens. Water containers and sacks of oranges, limes, and coconuts littered the top level. Chests, bales, and large earthen jars were piled everywhere. Smaller boats and canoes carrying a variety of fruits and vegetables floated alongside the already heavily loaded warship.

"Good day, Oyin." She said while passing.

"Not so." He stopped and approached her, "I saw a merchant selling your idol to a sick man."

"Impossible. Very few know about the powers of my idol," She said dismissingly.

"He was peddling its healing abilities." He gazed into her eyes. "It is not such a secret among our people. You may wish it as such, but it is not."

"Non-believers have no use for Santeria. Where is this sickly man?" She asked, knowing if it was true she had to speak to the man and retrieve it. "The gods must choose the owner. It cannot be stolen or bought."

"He is already aboard one of the fleet ships, they are setting sail at dawn. There is nothing you can do now."

"Back to work," an officer bellowed at him.

Foreigners crammed the cobblestone streets as Akanni made her way home. Her shrine looked disheveled and her statue for Olokun was missing. Weeks later news got back to Havana. A hurricane hit the fleet full force, destroying eleven of the ships and taking over 700 souls.

She knew her idol had fallen into the wrong hands.

CHAPTER FOURTEEN

JUNE 3, 2011

BIMINI

Lucas softly rocked me back and forth with his right hand, tenderly whispering, "Honey, wake up."

"What," I whispered, gradually opening my eyes. "Where are we?"

"Bimini Sands."

I glanced around the spacious indigo bedroom. A large painting portraying an endless field of bright yellow sunflowers came into view. On the other side of the room glass doors exposed a hint of morning light and offered a glimpse of the ocean through the curtains. I peeled the covers off me and felt my damp skin covered in sweat.

"I'm soaked. Feel my skin," I said, placing his hand on my chest.

"You were mumbling something about a portal."

"You can check out my portal," I teased.

He smiled, propped up on one elbow. "Honey, I'm worried about you. You were muttering it over and over, your eyes were fluttering and the heat you were radiating could melt an igloo."

"I'm sorry. I dreamed, and felt a powerful entity take over my body. I had no control, something else did. Sometimes I recall the details, other times I don't. But it seems to be a nightly theme, portals and idols and such." I remembered my magazine discovery, and all the chaos from yesterday. I turned my gaze toward him, "I read an interesting article about Santeria in Cuba and their religion and idols they worship. My nightmare probably stems from the story, the ghost ship, or the Bluewater sinking. I don't know."

"I think you're trying to get me to enter your portal in Cuba."

"Maybe," I giggled.

We played around and my dampness went from my skin to my groin. We quietly made love and for the first time in years the act felt like true love. The touch, the tenderness, affection and unspoken understanding. Afterward, we snuggled, finally deciding to get out of bed and face the day.

"*Carpe Diem.*" I mumbled, reminding me of a boat I spotted docking in Bimini last night named *Carpe Pescado*. Seize the fish, I imagined.

When we emerged upstairs, Russ sat on the balcony gazing toward the sea. Lucas watched FOX news while drinking his complimentary condo coffee. I grabbed some fresh brew, skipping the so called news for some natural serenity. I didn't feel like watching TV first thing in the morning. They were probably still talking about the oil spill. My honey would fill me in on Athena and her path.

"So, did you sleep well?" I asked Russ.

"I was still rocking from the boat and it rocked me right to sleep. And the rum helped."

I giggled. "I had fun at the beach club last night. The sushi tasted fresh."

"Well, I make better burgers, but those went down with the ship. But they did a decent job, besides it's the only restaurant on the south side of the island. We'll have to check out North Bimini for the experience. Perhaps this afternoon. It's a bit different, and full of history. I think you'll like it."

I smiled at him for considering my historical interest. "I'm game. I thought we had a few days? What's going on with the hurricane?"

"We're still in the cone of death and they're predicting a cat 2 by the five o'clock update. We'll be fine if we leave tomorrow. I'm not so sure about the following day." He looked me in the eyes, "I don't sail rough seas if I don't have to, and I certainly don't mess with Mother Nature."

I glanced back at the priceless view. The calm would change dramatically in the next few days if predictions were correct. The water seemed to dance with white sparks on the surface like handheld sparklers on the 4th of July. After our storm experience traversing the yellow bank, I knew the seas could turn violent in an instant, yet, I found it difficult to picture their ferociousness in this moment of tranquility.

I still sensed a heaviness hanging over Russ, an unspoken feeling of responsibility for the sinking of the Bluewater. It was an emotion he'd have to work through, but in my mind he did the best he could.

"Well, I'm going to run off all the beer I drank yesterday." Smiling, I said, "See you soon."

I silently passed Lucas who was engrossed in the TV, and knowing my routine he didn't even look up. I sauntered to a dirt road, walking while building up my energy and determination, eventually breaking into a jog. Lavender morning glories lined the path, shining upward to greet the sun. Dense scrub brush added a jungle-like feel to the tropical island.

Light peeked through the tall thin pine trees, creating an irregular pattern of shadows on the sandy trail. Buzzing crickets screamed through the trees at certain points and then complete silence. The only other noticeable sign of life was a few comical sideways moving land crabs. They'd raise a large claw in the air, attempting to intimidate and challenge another to a fight, all the while doing the horizontal tango into the road and back to the bush, proudly displaying an obscenely sizable claw. On a few occasions I had to stop and play with one of the arrogant little fellows, almost taunting him. Needless to say, I always won.

I stopped at the beach club to stretch, admiring the three-sided ocean view reflecting several shades of blue-green. Translucent cerulean and jade decorated the shallower waters, deep midnight to polar blue in the distance and a lighter sky blue in the forefront, a color I referred to as Bimini blue given its prominence in front of Bimini Sands and most of the island. It was perhaps the most beautiful luminous water I've ever seen. The multicolor ocean contrasted with a dilapidated rusting white fence and pink cement seawall with columns lining a small inlet allowing access to boating canals. Cement debris littered a beach rock jetty. A hurricane decimated the hotel in 2005, leaving only remnants behind. The set-back corner position of the beach club saved it. Between the dirt road where I stood, and the debris sat a solid row of sun drenched green bushes too lush and manicured to be native plants.

A small lawn patch Bermuda grass held indigenous sea-grape trees fashioned into spherical balls, strategically placed sunflowers, fuchsia bougainvillea, and a surfboard for ornamentation.

I was only fifteen minutes into my run and already drenched. I used my right hand, index finger side leading, to propel the sweat off my face like a windshield wiper during a downpour, a motion I continued through the remainder of my run.

South Bimini seemed quiet, although a few locals passed on golf carts with a quick flip of the hand. Golf doesn't exist on the island, but the cart seemed perfect for transportation given the island's small size and moderate climate. Not only were cars non-existent, except the scattered few, but also street signs, horns honking, background interstate noise, asphalt, squirrels, big lush trees, cats sitting on porches, lawn art and any sort of developed skyline.

On another side canal I jogged past private vacation homes belonging mostly to Americans. One and two-story homes mingled, some weathered, others appearing new. One small shack the size of a shipping container sat on stilts. A unique handmade wooden sign rested in the sandy yard of a lime green house. Wood arrows were nailed to a dock piling, pointing to Miami, a nude beach, Jamaica, Cozumel and Cuba. Where's the nude beach? I wondered, checking the arrow's direction with no mileage listed. Styrofoam nautical balls dangled below the bucolic signpost surrounded by oxygen tanks, boat bumpers, and conch shells.

I smelled wood burning, reminding me of Africa and the exotic experiences I had in Kenya and Tanzania many years ago. A ubiquitous charred wood aroma reminded me of the continent I loved the most, where I longed to live in my youth. Searching for the source of the scent I discovered a tree burning in the sand surrounded by scrub brush, apparently a controlled burn.

I found relief in a small marina pool, diving in and exhaling victory at the end of my painfully heated run. Hot yoga seemed easy compared to running in Bimini during the summer with a humid hurricane approaching. The air-conditioned condo felt like an igloo afterwards, so I quickly hit the shower.

Lucas stuck his head in. "Hey honey." He paused eyeing me up and down with an approving grin. "In about an hour, we're going to take the golf cart to the ferry and explore North Bimini. Right now Russ and I are going to the airport to check on the plane."

"You don't want to wait for me?" I asked.

"We'll be back soon. I just want to check on the fuel and make sure the keys are where Gary left them."

"I'll be ready when you get back."

Athena dominated the weather channel. It was just south of Turks and Caicos and heading toward the Bahamas with increasing wind speed and intensity. The hurricane hunters were deployed, but we wouldn't know the true category status until later in the afternoon. Locals on Turks and Caicos were putting up plywood on windows and preparing for a direct hit, although the storm might stay east of the island. Five possible tracks showed the hurricane going over most of the Bahamas with Bimini on three of the five. An animated reporter broadcast from West Caicos covering the different scenarios. It looked windy there but not too dramatic at the moment.

In Bimini, things seemed normal and relaxed, without a trace of a looming storm. Three boats were cruising the calm water out front and a few sunbathers dotted the beach. When the boys returned I mentioned the lack of concern in Bimini about the storm.

"Oh, this is pretty dead for Bimini in June," Lucas said, evenly. "Tomorrow will be a pivotal day for any tourists still left on the island. Let's go north, Russ is grabbing us a few beers."

Three locals were waiting for the water taxi accompanied by a single white goat.

I smiled warmly at the tropical setting complete with a five minute ride on a covered pontoon boat to the north side. I felt thousands of miles and decades away from the hustle and bustle of the states. On the ferry, I had a hard time following a conversation between two Bahamians, a thickly accented sing song dialect.

Russ had no problem conversing. "Yeah mon. Rain and wind all dah way. Everyting cool fa now." He swallowed a mouthful of beer.

"Ain't no big deal." One of them said and then "ya, ya, ya," and more rapidly something unrecognizable to my untrained ears, followed by a "Yeah, boy."

The pitch at the end of every word seemed to rise as if a question. I'd experienced it to different degrees throughout our journey, at different levels of inflection and speed. Slower speech helped my understanding.

We sauntered along the main dirt road, known as King's Road, in Alice Town where the ferry dropped us off. Vendors in the straw market along the way sold T-shirts, straw purses, coconut purses, sun dresses and knickknacks. Nothing peaked my interest, except for a woman who offered to French braid my hair.

"Ten dollars," She insisted, herding me into a chair.

"I don't know how to braid," I confessed.

"Easy, easy." She insisted, quickly weaving my hair from the crown to the nape of my neck.

The braid looked and felt good, keeping my hair off of my sweltering shoulders in the heat of the day. American money was as accepted as the Bahamian dollar, having an equal exchange value.

The guys lingered around the straw market, suggesting we stop at the End of the World bar for a beer.

Dark in comparison to the bright sun outside, the interior of the rustic tavern displayed writing all over wood panel walls, underwear hanging above, and signed currency from many countries taped on a panel behind the bar. Names of boats and fishing teams, individuals had signed with the dates they visited, relationships broadcasted, and love proclaimed.

"Interesting," I mumbled.

My name's in here," Lucas said.

"My underwear's on the ceiling," Russ challenged. I looked up searching for the camouflage boxers I saw earlier on the trip. Filled with mostly ladies' thongs, boxers also hung from above like flags revealing their conquest. My eyes shifted to one pair depicting a skull and crossbones with a patch over the eye, the typical Jolly Roger avatar faded and exposed. I briefly thought of Jeff and his treasure hunting *Davy Jones* yacht, wondering if they were still at Staniel Cay. I continued scanning for Russ's undies, my gaze landing on a pair representing the confederate flag, integrated among a rainbow of women's thongs. Blue, black, pick, multicolored, green and purple.

"That's yours," I pointed to the pair hanging in the distance. "The confederate flag, cowboy."

"Damn, you're good Raves. But wrong. I wouldn't give up a nice pair." He turned his stool in the opposite direction, pointing to a plain tan pair with grey scribblings. "Those are mine from 2001, when I was here on a wild fishing trip."

"So you let people sign your ass while wearing them, or

afterwards?" I asked, giggling at the thought of Russ running around the bar in his undies asking for autographs.

"On of course. A bunch of drunk girls in the bar. None on the front, of course. I'm not that type of guy."

I choked on my drink, spraying a mist of beer while laughing. "Oh, I could imagine." Glancing at Lucas, "So no undies on the ceiling for you, sweetie?"

Smirking, "No just a signature of my name and year, somewhere around here." His eyes scanned the tavern, searching for his dated autograph. He handed me a black sharpie, one of many sitting atop the bar. "Make your mark," he said.

Eagerly grabbing the sharpie and searching for an empty section to claim as my own, I noticed fainter scratching's were written over with darker, fresher markings. I avoided busy walls and found a corner behind a speaker and wrote, *Raven and Lucas, Breakfast in Bimini, 2011.* Satisfied, I joined the two men sitting on bar stools, gulping a slightly stronger Kalik gold.

"Ok, now the undies," Russ blurted out, wickedly grinning.

"And I can do a shot from your belly button," Lucas added with an equally sinful grin. "It's tradition in this bar."

I addressed both of them with an unwavering "Oh, I don't think so," delivered with a polite smile. "But I'd have to say, this place definitely has character."

"You might change your mind after a few of these," Lucas said, handing me a beer to go.

Apparently, walking the streets of Bimini with a beverage is also traditional. We leisurely headed to the Big Game Club for lunch. Strolling past some ruins, we stopped for a moment of nostalgia. Lucas and Russ enthusiastically talked about the colorful history the *Compleat Angler.*

"Ernest Hemingway slept, drank and wrote here in the 1930's." Lucas said.

"And my favorite, Jimmy Buffett," Russ said, "He even sat in with the local band. And Gary Hart got caught messing around at the bar and hotel during his presidential campaign. I know I've had my share of debauchery here."

"Me too," Lucas admitted.

"No, not you two." I teased. Listening to them reminisce drunken adventures as if a competition for the raunchiest tale. However, neither had accepted a blow job from the toothless island hooker. *Thank god*, I silently rejoiced.

"It was packed every weekend." Russ said. "Stevie S playing in one corner, drinks flowing at the bar and through a small opening into the dance room. Even the small Hemingway room overflowed."

Now only a brick fireplace stood in the center of boulders outlining three rooms and an outside patio. An A-frame wooden sign over a stone archway read *The Compleat Angler*, a reminder of its humble yet vibrant past.

"How did it burn down? Do you think they'll rebuild it?" I asked.

Continuing our stroll along King's Road, cowboy snickered exhaling an explanation. "The fire was questionable, and the owner was the only one who died. It destroyed all the Hemingway memorabilia. Lots of gossip about foul play followed, but no arrests were made."

"With its popularity, why not make a historic replica?"

Lucas took a swig from his beer. "It's the Bahamas, nothing much gets done around here."

Russ agreed, nodding. "At least not fast. Besides, I don't think they have the desire or resources."

"Hmm." I said. "It sounds like a great opportunity for foreign investment. Build it and they will come."

Russ smiled, glancing in my direction. "Easy for you to say. I don't even know who owns the land, I guess the family of the deceased owner, but land ownership is different here than in the states." He took a sip of beer. "I'd like to hang out there again."

"Me too. Or maybe I could just watch you run around in your undies at the End of the World bar."

He cast a half glance and a smirk in my direction, holding back a sarcastic innuendo, I presumed.

The Big Game Club is a humble resort resembling a roadhouse motel with an upgraded pool, large marina and a spacious, airy restaurant overlooking the docks. We sat outside so Lucas and I could smoke while admiring the dreamy view. I lit a cigarette, hoping to sour the scent of fried food lingering in the air since our arrival in Alice Town. I studied the menu listing French fries, fried fish, fried conch fritters, bacon cheeseburgers, pretty much everything soaked in oil. I half expected fried Oreos and Twinkies under the dessert section, like a state fair with artery-clogging grub.

I spotted a salad on the menu, described as having lettuce, nuts, strawberries, cucumbers, and feta. They also had grilled cheese, but I imagined cheesy bread also being deep fried, so I ordered the greens I craved.

A handful of boats floated in the marina, most appearing unoccupied. I spotted three young men near a center console named *Fishy Whipped*. They were cleaning and bagging fish, casually throwing small carcasses into the water. Undulating in the calm waves, two nurse sharks benefitted from their morning catch. A baby blue heron stood on the dock eagerly eyeing scraps. One of the boys, a tanned stocky yellow-haired guy, occasionally tossed a piece of meat sideways in the heron's direction, who gobbled it up midair.

Smiling at the friendly sharing, I pointed, inventing a nickname for the bird. "Look at the cute blue heron. Let's call it Fish Face."

"You're naming animals?" Russ asked with a sideways glance.

"Well, yes. *Fishy Whipped* is feeding Fish Face."

He rolled his eyes. "Okay, pescatarian."

The guys were more interested in the type of fish. Snapper, yellow tail snapper they agreed, and maybe a mutton or two. Our food and another round of beer arrived. A warm breeze increased to about ten knots reminding me of the idol I found during the west wind just weeks prior. I wondered what additional artifacts I could find roaming the beach after lunch, once we took the short boat ride to South Bimini. Perhaps the sea could reveal more clues to the statue's identity. In less than twenty-four hours we'd be back in Florida with more research opportunities.

I heard an engine rumble growing louder, not quite sounding like a boat. Lucas pointed past the marina, "It's a seaplane."

My heart palpitated with excitement. I admired all aircraft, but seaplanes really thrilled me, somehow screaming exotic adventure in my mind. The blue and white Cessna on floats landed perfectly in front of the Big Game Club. Not skipping a beat between landing and rollout, splaying water in its path.

"Awesome." I blurted out, my heart still racing. "Where does the plane go now to disembark?"

"It has two options," Russ answered after a quick bite of a conch fritter. "The old Chalk's landing ramp is just down the road to the west, or it can pull up to any dock."

The plane drifted like a sea-duck, finding a final resting place at a far end dock where two passengers and a pilot disembarked. Lucas's attention shifted inside to a TV above the bar. CNN was reporting strong winds and rain slamming Turks and Caicos. The guys scrambled indoors to get a better view of the top story.

I stayed at our table, enjoying a post lunch cigarette while taking in the serene beauty for a lingering few minutes. I noticed an Azimut resembling the *Davy Jones* at a distant dock. Shit, my palms got sweaty.

Walking inside I noticed Lucas and Russ energetically exchanging words and hand movements, their eyes flitting toward the TV. They were drawing pictures on a napkin, small ink blots and several messy lines.

"Everyone on the island who can leave should." Lucas urged. "The highest point on the island is only 18 feet."

Russ shook his head. "I don't think it'll be a direct hit, but a wobble left or right of the island. Windy, but not the center."

"Either way, we have to leave tomorrow. It's a gamble not to, like betting your life on a single hand, hoping the odds are in your favor." Lucas said. "Russ, can you gas up the Intrepid as soon as we return to South Bimini?" He turned towards me, "Raves and I will get our flight filed, and call weather brief and customs."

"So does the plane have enough fuel?" I asked.

"Yes, we checked this morning. We have thirty gallons, more than enough. And the keys are near the oil dipstick."

"If it didn't have fuel, you'd be shit out of luck," Russ added. "They don't have avgas on this island."

We were getting another beer and paying our bill when Jenny and Jeff appeared at the bar. "Are you following us?" I asked, only half joking.

Jenny giggled. "We're heading to Miami. We figured it'd be a good time to get boat maintenance done. And Jeff has a bit of web work, the possibility of us being without internet for weeks on Staniel seemed pretty high."

I raised my eyebrows and glanced at Lucas. "So you hightailed it to Bimini?"

"Pretty much." She said. "We're leaving for Florida tomorrow."

"Raves, I'm sorry about my behavior the other night." Jeff said sheepishly. "I had a bit too much rum."

"No worries," I fibbed. I didn't trust him, or his reasons for going to Florida. "Have you ever heard of the *SS Cotopaxi?*"

"It's a tramp freighter that disappeared in the 1920's in the Bermuda Triangle. Why? Does this relate to your artifact?"

"No. I just read something about it recently."

"Come on Raves, we have to go." Lucas said, nudging my side. "Bye Jenny and Jeff," he mumbled, acknowledging them for the first time. "Good luck."

"Are you guys staying on the *Cabin Fever*?" Jenny called out.

"Yes." Lucas lied.

The commuter boat unloaded a few passengers, and then we hopped aboard for a brief crossing southbound. Our complimentary condo-provided golf cart sat among a scattered few where we left it. After dropping off Russ to refuel the Intrepid, we sidetracked through an area located within Bimini Sands known as 'the boneyard.' Several rusted freight cars housing tools and building supplies sat alongside decomposing cars, trucks, boats and construction equipment littering the sandy terrain. A few boats resting on trailers were completely intact, belonging to homeowners who stored their vessels there. When they returned it was an easy drop into the marina. A rooster and three chicks cooed, strutting among the debris. Picking up pace to avoid our approaching golf cart, hatchlings dutifully followed the hen's direction and speed.

"This is where vehicles come to die," Lucas said.

"It's rustic. Island style quaint."

"Boneyard," I heard myself say upon reflection. I briefly remembered excavating hundreds of skeletons in a true boneyard, so for me it held a different meaning.

Our dying golf cart sluggishly crawled back to the condo where Lucas plugged it into the electric outlet. On the balcony we listened to the marine forecast on the handheld VHF. The mechanical male voice broadcasted.

Hazardous weather outlook for coastal Florida Atlantic waters. Tonight, wind NE 15 to 20 knots, seas 6 to 8 feet with occasional seas to 10 feet in the Gulf Stream, small craft advisory. Tuesday, mostly sunny becoming partly cloudy in the afternoon. Wind NE 20 to 25 knots, seas 8 to 10 feet with occasional seas to 13 feet. Sea surface temperature 87 degrees. Wednesday, mostly cloudy. Wind NE 23 to 30 knots, seas 12 to 15 feet with occasional seas to 18 feet. Sea surface temperature 87 degrees. Thursday, chance of tropical storm and/ or hurricane conditions.

Despite the monotone warning, I started to panic for unrelated reasons. I lit a cigarette, standing against the railing, "It sounds like we have a tailwind for our flight. Is Russ okay boating by himself tomorrow? The winds and water seem pretty strong and dire. Should he fly with us?"

Lucas also grabbed a cigarette, lighting it with a murmured response. "Russ will have a choppy ride, but he's an experienced captain."

"When are we departing? Do you want me to fly?" I wanted to be in control, flying while he navigated, so I clarified, "I'd like to be in the left seat,"

He inhaled smoke followed by an affectionate exhale in my direction. "Yes, you can be captain. And I think we should shoot for a ten o'clock departure, what do you think?" He asked.

I considered an earlier departure given the weather, quickly realizing our Bahamian-style, no problem mon, everything will be good lifestyle the past few weeks and answered, "Sounds good." Besides, I could take a quick morning run to clear my head prior to our flight.

Staring out to sea I noticed a small boat wiggling near the shoreline, just slightly larger than a canoe. Sitting towards the rear a local Biminite maneuvered a mini outboard engine producing a constant hum. A mound of pink conch shells were piled in the center. The dinghy appeared soiled on the inside, a permanent grime staining its stark white interior. In the distance three red and three green buoys, resembling colored pawns on a chess board, bobbed on top of the water, signaling the boat entry channel.

Red, meant right when returning from the ocean, I remembered Lucas saying. I noticed waves breaking on a sandbar in the shallower aquamarine as whitecaps danced on the Gulf Stream's surface.

"Let's go to the marina," He called from inside. "Russ should be tying up soon."

Strolling arm in arm to the dock as if being escorted into a ballroom dance, we approached Russ attempting to rope the dock piling as if it was a mustang and he was a cowboy in a rodeo. He missed so Lucas grabbed the other end of the line, pulling the Intrepid to the tie down.

"Nice try cowboy," I teased.

He shot me a sideways glance. "You'd better watch out, or I'll try my lassoing skills on your ass.

"Ha," I dismissed, not wanting to challenge him, although it sounded exciting.

"We have a problem," he said directing his gaze at Lucas. "There's no fuel here or on the north."

"What? Are you sure?" Lucas said.

"I spoke with the dockmaster. The north sold out days ago, and they sent everyone to Bimini Sands. The sands ran out earlier today. Due to Athena, the fuel barge wouldn't arrive until the storm passes."

Lucas paced the dock. I could almost see his mind rotating like a jet engine. "How much fuel do we have?"

"Forty gallons. I can't make it with less than sixty on a calm day, but I really need a hundred with the seas."

"The boats stored in the boneyard should have clean fuel. We need to syphon some." He pointed to the red canister on the stern. "Grab the gas can Russ. We'll take the golf cart." Looking at me, "Raves can you find a clear glass from the condo and meet us at the boneyard."

I ran to the condo, found a glass, and hurried back where the guys were waiting near the first boat we'd syphon.

The container only held six gallons, meaning many trips back and forth. Lucas drained a minuscule amount into the glass. "Looks good," he declared.

After filling the can, he handed it to Russ. "Raves, go with Russ so you can run the container between the two of us."

"Come-on Russ, I'll drive the golf cart." It was a short ride followed by quick pace to the boat.

After he emptied its contents into the fuel tank, I grabbed the red can. "I'll be back."

Back in the boneyard, Lucas tensely said. "I'm having a hard time finding fuel. Barely any in the boats I've found so far. One seemed to have plenty bad fuel."

"Do you think someone already syphoned these?"

His t-shirt appeared drenched in sweat and he smelled like a gas station. "I don't know. I have enough from this boat for another run or two. I'll check a few more while you're gone."

I returned to Russ who seemed busy organizing the boat. Fishing rods, tackle box, and towels were stored in the head and the cooler securely bungeed underneath the leaning post. Charts were folded and placed in the radio box overhead.

"Round two," I announced, not wanting to alarm him of a

possible fuel shortage.

I found Lucas at the same spot, "Any luck?" I asked.

"Nope. We have one more from this boat. The rest are dry or dirty." He filled the container almost to the top, and then nothing. He tried to rock the small vessel for another few drops. It was dry.

"Can we give him some of our Avgas from the plane?" I asked.

He lit up and smiled. "That's a possibility, and a great idea."

Back at the boat, Lucas handed Russ the canister. "I have good news and bad news, which do you want first?"

"I'll take the good." Russ replied.

"We have fuel, but we have to go to the airport. This is the last from the boats. The rest are empty and I suspect already syphoned."

"I'm at fifty-eight gallons." Russ said. "I'd be comfortable with another ten to twenty. So if you have it on the plane, let's go."

"Raven, you didn't leave your idol on this boat, did you?" Russ called out.

"No, it's in my duffle bag. I'll take it on the plane."

"Good. I don't need any bad juju out there tomorrow." He paused. "In fact, you may want to leave it on the island where you found it."

I snickered and inaudibly whispered, "Not a chance."

CHAPTER FIFTEEN

JUNE 3, 2011

BIMINI, BAHAMAS

We passed the shark lab on our way to the beach club, prompting me to recall my morning jog desire to visit. "We didn't tour the shark lab."

"Next time," Lucas said from the driver's seat. "We'll be back again later this summer."

"I can't wait. It's such a quaint island." Our time here seemed effortless and timeless. I imagined losing track of days, weeks or even months. My body felt covered in dust from the dirt roads and lack of rain, like I'd been through a haboob.

A few scattered locals convened around the bar, glancing up at our arrival and then back at the TV's. After ordering a seafood pizza, we played the hook game. The bartender kept the wine, rum, and vodka flowing, as we soaked it up with a tasty pie between games. Russ won the most rounds with three and Lucas tied my two hooks. A local challenged Russ to a game, noticing his wins and betting him a beer. He appeared to be middle-aged, but trendy with blondish tinted dreadlocks and a single gold-capped front tooth. He smelled dusty with a wood-spice cologne mist. Standing with his back against the fishhook, he blindly held the loop to his forehead and stepped away. Geometry, propulsion and sway carried the circle to the wall, successfully pegging about half his shots. The three of us watched in amazement. Russ scored four out of ten, turned down a second challenge and bought the man a beer.

"Next," Russ announced in a defeated tone.

I confiscated the hook, just as a stranger approached for a challenge.

"I'll play," he said.

He wore a baseball cap with a Cayce foundation logo, a short grey beard, faded Levis, and a plain black t-shirt. I handed him the hook. "Best of ten," I offered.

"Cayce foundation? As in Edgar Cayce?" I asked.

"Yes. I'm here researching the Bimini Road."

My eyes widened as I unhooked his first hit from the wall, walking the circle back to him. "What kind of research?"

"We conducted a mag survey to see if we could find anything unusual in the area. A mag survey is…"

Cutting him short, "I'm an archaeologist. I'm familiar with the method."

He scratched his scruffy beard, hooking the fishhook again. "My background is parapsychology and I'm an Atlantean scholar. I've worked with a few archaeologists over the years."

He offered his right hand, firmly shaking mine. "I'm Henry."

"Raves." I said with a toasty smile. I couldn't believe my luck. I wanted to know everything about Atlantis, and why and how somebody could think an ancient advanced European civilization existed in such a remote part of the world.

"So what did you find?" We forgot about the game, sitting on nearby bar stools. Lucas delivered me a glass of white wine, quickly returning to his clique.

"Well, the activity looks promising. The survey results show a high concentration of debris. My divers are concentrating on exploring this area over the next few months."

"Any artifacts or evidence? What are you hoping to discover?"

"The Pillars of Hercules would be nice, or a stele reading *nec plus ulta.*" He paused watching me with piercing ice blue eyes. "Cayce predicted Poseida as the first portion of Atlantis to rise again, around 1968-69. Poseidon resides over the island between the pillars of Hercules."

He sounded cult-like, passionately steadfast in his conviction.

"*Nec plus ulta?*"

"Nothing further beyond. A warning to sailors."

My heart palpated. The stele in my dream read "Nothing further beyond." Could it have been an Atlantean warning?

Although I believed Atlantis to be a fable, I needed to know more. I'd already reconsidered many of my previously held convictions in the past week, especially after finding the captain's log aboard the *SS Cotopaxi*.

Taking a swig from my wine, I asked him. "Can you fill me in on Atlantis? I know the basics...but what exactly is Atlantis supposed to look like?"

He beamed, proud to share his knowledge. "11,500 years ago an advanced society flourished, an island empire the size of Libya and Asia combined. Protected by Poseidon, Atlanteans grew more powerful until their ethics declined. For punishment, earthquakes and floods inundated the island, and it sunk into the Atlantic Ocean, taking with it the warriors, temples, and every trace of such an evolved race."

I nodded, caught Lucas's eye signaling two fingers for a round of drinks for Henry and myself.

He continued. "Poseidon's home was surrounded by three rings of land with bridges allowing people to cross over to his central palace. They had harbors and canals connecting to the sea where they'd receive vessels from afar."

He spoke enthusiastically as if he considered the Greek god a real and close relative. I suppressed my disbelief for the moment and listened.

"The circular walls of his temple were covered in tin, brass, silver, gold and orichalcum. His innermost temple held many statues, including a charioteer of six winged horses, and stelai invoking curses on the disobedient. They used crystals extensively, because of their ability to transfer energy."

I thought of the crystal lodged in Uga-Bugga's head. "What kind?"

"They had crystals in every color, each with specific qualities, harnessing different energy. Pink crystals were known for their healing potential. They provided great amounts of power in a short period of time. Cancer, blood diseases and other ailments could be easily removed in Atlantis." He scratched his beard. "I held one once. It radiated immense energy."

No way in hell I would tell him about my idol with its embedded pink crystal. I imagined him killing me for it.

"Do they emit any glow?" I asked.

"The powerful ones do, and it's said the most powerful crystal radiates a green glow, becoming brighter when it activates its abilities."

My eyes widened. "What kind of abilities?"

"It's capable of transmitting energy across space and time." He said matter-of-factly.

"So, time-travel?"

He smiled. "So much more. They used and redirected energy all around the universe. Ultimately, carelessly misusing the great crystal resulted in the destruction and sinking of Atlantis.

Lucas delivered our drinks. "Honey, this is Henry. He's researching the Bimini Road." Facing him I silently lipped, "No idol talk."

"Pleased to meet you," he said, then retreated back to the bar joining Russ and a few others. I decided to share my stele Africa dream. "I had this dream the other day. I was in Africa at a voodoo ceremony and in the middle of the arena sat a stele inscribed *'nothing further beyond'.*

His intense blue-eyed stare made me squirm. "You really dreamed that?" he asked.

"Yes. I sometimes have a crazy imagination, but I wouldn't make it up. And I've had dreams of portals and vortexes. It's kinda weird." I didn't dare mention the statue.

"It means you're a descendant of the Atlantean race."

I scoffed.

"Cayce had similar dreams. He knew he lived in Atlantis in a past life, one of the reasons he's considered one of the greatest psychics, he could recall memories from the ancient civilization and pinpointed its location off of Bimini." He took a sip of beer, continuing. "The Isle of Poseida is the planet's most potent vortex portal complex. Its energies are calling you back."

"I have a mix of many genes, but I'm sure Atlantean isn't one. And I'm not convinced it's "calling me back." Did I believe in otherworldly energies? From what I'd seen recently, yes. But when it came to Atlantis, I'd certainly need more proof. Not just some random parapsychologist telling me I was from an ancient culture I didn't believe existed. I wanted to share the idol discovery with him, but decided to remain silent about it and my other nightmares, things I imagined he'd interpret as prophecies.

"I think Lucas is calling me. Let's go to the bar and I'll give you my email. I'd love to explore Bimini Road next time we visit. We

Breakfast in Bimini

have to leave tomorrow because of the hurricane. Are you?"

"No. I'll ride it out. I think it'll be a weak one."

Did he too think he had psychic powers? A descendant of the Atlantean race? We strolled to the bar where I scribbled my email on a napkin. Henry, Lucas and Russ exchanged handshakes and we got a drink to go. Henry handed me his card with all his contact information.

The card read *Henry Ferro. Atlantean Scholar, researcher and enthusiast.* A logo depicting a flying dove declared, *Edgar Cayce's A.R.E. Association for Research and Enlightenment. Your Body, Mind, Spirit Resources since 1931.*

"Wow, he's a bit wacky. A parapsychologist is just a fancy word for a kooky nut." I said as we left the bar.

Lucas blinked at me, not quite understanding. "Why? What did you talk about?"

"He's an Atlantean scholar studying the Bimini Road. I thought I'd pick his brain on the subject."

"Perfect for you." Russ interjected.

"Well, I shared one of my dreams with him, and he thinks my ancestors were from Atlantis, and that's why I have special dreams and prophecies. Because Atlantean is in my blood."

"That explains your pescatarian ways," Russ said.

Lucas giggled, prompting Russ into a full cackle. It was contagious and I laughed at myself.

Outside I noticed a glow on the horizon resembling Neapolitan ice cream with the ocean as dark chocolate, a blurred strawberry twinkle and vanilla glow in the sky. Pointing toward the distant sea, "What's the light over there?"

"The glow of Miami." Lucas answered. "It's a constant light you can see from Bimini most nights. I visited here after hurricane Andrew and it was completely dark in the distance. A bit eerie when you're used to seeing the glimmer."

"Wow, fifty miles and it's still visible. Kinda like Vegas when driving from the desert." I pointed to bright light low in the sky. "That looks too low to be a star."

"It's a light on the top of the sailboat honey."

Squinting, I could barely make out the outline of a sailboat anchored off the beach club. Even with the Miami glow, the ocean appeared dark, like a sea of oil with no transparency on this moonless night.

On the cart ride back, my gaze shifted from the glow in the east to the radiant stars above and to the west. The big dipper and Orion appeared bright, with the three sisters clearly visible. Pointing upwards, I said, "Orion is above us and in the center of its belt is a nebula."

"A what?" Russ asked from the back seat.

I turned towards him. "A nebula. You can even see the reddish tint. The three stars in a row are part of Orion's belt and it's known as the three sisters. The center star is actually a nebula. A colorful cloud of gas and dust where new stars are formed." Secretly, I hoped my memory from astronomy class held true, but somehow suspected neither Russ nor Lucas would know the difference.

Pointing to the west I said, "There's the Big Dipper." And then to the southwest "And Canis Major."

"We can see them better from the airport. It's really dark out there." Lucas said.

Russ shot back, "No, we need a good night's rest. Tomorrow will be an early and possibly taxing day."

On the ride back, I caught a glimpse of a shooting star. *I'll save my wish*, I decided.

In the middle of the night I imagined walking towards a luminescent green light, radiating more brightly with each gentle step. I wasn't frightened, but strong and confident. Walking through the emerald glow I encountered three large concentric rings alternating water and land. Effortlessly roaming past the circles to a center I found a large golden statue of a muscular, bearded man holding a pitchfork. The statue spoke to me saying, "The portal is beneath you." I slowly turned around back through the light. Briefly awaking and radiating heat, I promptly tossed the comforter onto Lucas and fell back to sleep.

CHAPTER SIXTEEN

JUNE 4, 2011

BIMINI, BAHAMAS

The winds howled at daybreak. Gently pulling back the curtains, I watched colossal waves splash against the shoreline, turning into foam. I twisted toward Lucas peacefully snuggled in a fetal position, and softly announced, "Good morning honey."

His eyelashes gradually revealed half of his green eyes, his lips turning upward in recognition. "Hi sweetie." He blinked and repositioned himself. "Sounds like decent sized waves and wind out there."

"Yeah, it's pretty. But not for Russ. I heard him milling about upstairs."

"Let's go see him off," he said while getting out of bed.

I sipped my coffee a little too quickly listening to the two of them discussing details of the crossing.

"I should arrive in port Everglades in about three hours." Russ said. "I'll have a following sea. I already crosschecked all equipment and radios and I have plenty of flares." He paused for clarification. "I won't need them, but just in case, so you can spot me from the air if you follow the same heading."

Lucas confirmed, "We'll follow the same heading about 10:30. You should be close to the port by then. If we don't hear from you by 12:30, we'll call the coast guard and start our own search."

Athena was now in the southern part of the Exuma Sound just

northeast of Long Island, and classified a category 2 with sustained winds of 105 mph. The forecast called for a category 3 by the next day, when it would head north through the Bahamas.

We helped untie the boat and watched Russ depart from the inlet to the west northwest for Fort Lauderdale. The bow of the boat plunged into the sea, sending a wall of water into the hull, drenching Russ in the mist.

"Ouch," I heard myself say. Then he went full throttle onto a plane, disappearing over the horizon.

"That's the best way to do it," Lucas said wryly. "Full speed ahead."

My jog took me along the same path as the day before. The beach club and a side canal, although this time any sweat I produced instantly dried in the wind. I thought about my strange dream, it wasn't a nightmare, I didn't feel intimidated or uneasy. But the talking statue holding a pitchfork seemed a bit odd, as did the lucid green glow. The pitchfork must have been a trident which meant Poseidon, the Greek god of the sea, warning me about a portal beneath me.

Atlantis has risen, I thought. If I shared this dream with Henry, he'd probably agree.

Although windy, the protected marina appeared calm, the water perfectly transparent and the sun as intense as ever. I bought a water from the Ship's Shore with the two dollars I had stuffed in the pocket of my running shorts.

Underneath a sign on the dock reading *Shark-free Marina*, with a red circle and line going through a generic shark, floated a small nurse shark. I guess the nurse didn't get the memo, I thought. Quite a few tiny fish gathered in the protected waters as I walked back to our rented condo. I noticed the stripes on one fish the size of my forefinger, a non-threatening baby barracuda. My eyes zoomed in on a small patch of floating grass. It took a moment, but a pocket-sized seahorse came into view, mingling with the weeds. It was my first time seeing one in nature. It looked adorable, almost cuddly. A single sailboat remained in the otherwise deserted harbor.

At the airport we did a preflight inspection. I checked the fuel by draining and inspecting a sample, making sure no water existed, and then I dipped a plastic fuel gauge into the tank.

"Eighteen gallons is enough, right?"

"Yes."

Lucas loaded our bags, checked the oil and did a walk around. A low-winged Piper Cherokee six rolled down the runway. A charter flight carrying six eagerly waiting passengers and a black Labrador prepared to leave. Only three other planes sat on the tarmac. One lacked a propeller, another had both wings removed, and the last one had two flat tires and a faded paint job. A tall, thin mechanic dressed in navy blue pants and a t-shirt worked on the plane missing the prop. I smiled at the exoticness of the quaint non-towered airport.

We departed on runway 8, climbing and turning to the northeast tip of Bimini and then over the rough waters in the Atlantic. Lucas stayed on radios as I flew. He had a hard time reaching Miami Center for flight following so he switched between Miami Departure and Miami Center with the frequencies he wrote down. I kept our heading at 330 degrees, leveling off at 4500 feet, checking all the instruments. Everything looked good, in the green. Suddenly, the oil pressure needle swung extreme right, into the red.

"Honey, the oil pressure is at maximum," I said through my microphone.

His eyes widened as he fidgeted with the instrument panel, tapping and flicking the oil pressure gage, hoping it was just stuck.

"The oil temperature looks..." He started to say, until the plane fell silent, the propeller stopping midflight.

"Should I head back to Bimini?" I asked. I raised the plane's nose, trading speed for a higher altitude, leveling off at the recommended best glide speed of 75 knots.

"No, we're too far, almost halfway to Florida."

"MAYDAY, MAYDAY." Lucas called, frantically switching radio frequencies between Miami Departure and Miami Center, trying to reach anyone as our altitude slowly decreased.

I picked up the engine out checklist, keeping my eye on the airspeed. I tried to restart, checking the magnetos, fuel selector, and fuel pump. Nothing but eerie silence filled the air. "Fly the airplane, you can do this," I said faintly. Talking to air traffic control was my least concern, but a very real one for Lucas. He concentrated on how we'd be rescued, while I focused on surviving an imminent crash into the ocean. I frantically reviewed everything on my checklist again, preparing for a ditch.

Lucas made one last feeble attempt to reach Miami,

"MAYDAY, MAYDAY. This is 8547 Whiskey going down twenty miles northwest of Bimini. MAYDAY." Lucas released control of the radio. He reached for a life vest, placing it around my neck and then securing one around his own.

"I love you baby," he said with sincerity.

"Oh, baby I love you too." My voice sounded a bit shaky. It wasn't the ideal setting to exchange our first declaration of love, but it might be our only chance

"Just pretend like you're landing on a runway." I told myself over and over trying to be convincing as Lucas counted down our altitude. "Fifty feet to go. Hold on."

I applied principles I'd learned in flight school. Keep the angle steady with slight adjustments up or down until touchdown. Without power, there was no room for mistakes. The angle controlled speed, if too low it would stall, causing the plane to stop gliding and drop out of the sky. A perfect landing is just a stall a few feet above the surface and I aced it for a hard but upright landing.

I already had the door unlatched, with my flip-flop wedged in the slight opening to provide for an easy escape. Immediately releasing my seatbelt, I swung the door open, glancing over to Lucas, who trailed right behind me with a red life raft in his right hand. Leaping into the ocean I felt slightly relieved, at least we landed safely and were both alive. The plane didn't flip, a real concern with fixed gear.

After pulling the cord to inflate my life jacket, I started kicking my legs, bobbing around in the choppy Gulf Stream. Lucas struggled to release the life raft, which had caught in the door. As we worked to get the inflatable untangled, I noticed blood streaming from a gash on his temple. Not wanting to alarm him, I stayed silent. Not only could his injury be more serious than it looked, but could also attract sharks. In the Gulf Stream several types roamed, including the deadly whitetip we'd encountered a few days before. Thoughts of the wreck of the Indianapolis crossed my mind, and I prayed we'd not become another statistic of a deadly shark attack.

"Damn raft's stuck between the seat and the door." He yanked his arm around on the inside of the cockpit. "It's caught on something. The seat track, I think."

I steadily moved my legs back and forth, in quick thrusts. "I'll climb inside and try to free it?"

"No, it's too dangerous. Water is rapidly flowing into the cockpit." He grunted and tugged with one hand, the other straining to keep the door open.

I tried to propel myself towards him to help, but I found myself drifting farther away. I kicked full force, barely inching closer to the plane.

His arm vigorously tugged and he groaned louder. He yelled, with one powerful pull. "I got it."

Kicking around the deep ocean Lucas struggled to open the inflatable while drifting away from the wreckage. His blood steadily trickled into the water like a dripping faucet.

"Do you need help?" I asked with a slightly shaky voice. "Honey, what can I do?" I kicked faster and harder. I finally reached him.

He grunted. "It's opening. But, I think…I think it might have a tear in it." The raft slowly unraveled. The sides expanded as the middle sank.

Looking over at the Cessna I saw only the tip of the tail above water. "There goes the plane and Uga-Bugga," I mumbled. *I guess the idol found its way home, deep in the sea. Forever gone, along with everything else.*

The ocean's expanse seemed larger and looking over Lucas's shoulder so did the fin I saw coming towards us.

"Sweets jump into the raft, now!" He hesitated, afraid to lose the buoyancy of the raft. "Honey a shark is heading towards us. Now please." I leaped onto the side and Lucas dove onto the other side. Our bodies were out of the water, but I didn't think the raft would hold us for long.

A ten foot shark slowly circled us. "That's a whitetip," Lucas said with conviction as he moved farther inside our inflatable boat. Our raft resembled a donut. The sides were completely inflated, but it had a big hole in the center. The midpoint tear was the size of a tennis ball, big enough to keep the area surrounding the gash submerged. Blood from Lucas's head continuously dripped into the water.

"Sweets. Why don't you lie on your back and let your head rest," I said, hoping his blood would coagulate. "You're bleeding a little."

"A whitetip is about to bump us and you want me to lay down."

I shimmied out of my shirt and gave it to him. "At least put this over your head," I said, leaning over and handing it to him. He balanced himself with his legs and one arm while tying the cloth around the wound.

I looked at the donut hole, noticing only an inch or so of water swishing around the bottom. My stomach pressed tightly to the inner part of the raft, my arms and legs wrapped around its top.

"Hold on," he shouted.

I hugged the boat like an infant being taken from its mother. My body completely enveloped the rounded edge of the raft. The bump felt like a strong push, not enough to dislodge me. Lucas apparently did the same. I relaxed my grip slightly. For the first time since our oceanic ditch I audibly exhaled and then smiled.

He grinned back. "Why are you smiling?"

"Because we are still both on the raft; we are still alive—and I think we are going to live through this." He scanned all directions for the shark's fin. I wondered out loud, "Do you think ATC heard our mayday?"

His grasp on the boat relaxed a bit as he took turns looking at me and the ocean. "It's possible they heard us and we didn't hear them. Hell anything's possible right now. We filed a flight plan and notified customs. They should know we are missing in the next few hours." I noticed his face turn grim again. "The shark is back."

"Did he bring friends," I said, trying to make light of our situation. "The hole in the bottom of the boat is not too big, should we try to sit inside?" I inquired.

His eyes followed the fin in the distance. He quickly glanced at the center of the boat then back into the water. "It's too risky. Oceanic whitetips are known for attacking from the bottom and it could easily bite through the thin rubber." He glimpsed at the donut hole again then at me. "And our weight could increase the water flow." His eyes darted around looking for the shark. I noticed his grip on the raft tighten. The concern in his eyes made me tense and I copied him.

"Hold on."

It struck the bottom of the boat, a large hump momentarily displacing the water. Jolting us side to side, we firmly held on for our lives. I couldn't grip any tighter and I felt like my short fingernails would puncture the raft. I saw the shark's shadow cruise away.

"Don't be fooled." Lucas said. "He'll probably be back. The damn bastard probably has nothing better to do."

I scanned the Atlantic, noticing its deep violet color radiating light from the reflection of the intense sun. The swells were gentle and almost relaxing, but the shark and constant choppy waters kept us both on edge. Beyond, Athena loomed, causing higher than normal winds and seas.

"Honey, how many feet do you think the waves are right now?"

"About six. They'll increase as the day goes on."

"Well, we'll be rescued by then." I stayed positive, although I wasn't convinced anyone heard our call for help. But we had hope, and each other.

I closed my eyes, pretending I was drifting in the Bimini Sands marina. I tasted the salty air, realizing I was thirsty. Dried salt water left a sticky residue over every inch of my body and stiffened my clothes. I suddenly craved fresh water, a desire I couldn't satisfy. Trying to forget my dehydration, I looked around the ocean again for any signs of the shark or life in general. I didn't see the shark fin, but imagined he still patrolled the vicinity. The thought of a really dangerous shark stalking us made me shiver. A flying fish whizzed by just feet above the water. I smiled and my lips cracked.

I turned to Lucas, "Sweets, why don't you relax a bit and rest your head. I don't see the shark."

"That concerns me even more," he said as he repositioned my shirt on his head. "Is my head still bleeding?" he asked.

I couldn't tell with the dark brown color of the shirt so I suggested, "Why don't you dip it in the salt water and put it back on your head. Salt water heals. Right now it's the best thing to do, along with resting."

Lucas rinsed the shirt in the center of the boat, wrung it out and tied it back on his head. He placed his head and nape on the raft's rim, facing me and sighing. "You know with the wind direction and current we won't hit land, not in the Gulf Stream. Not until Africa."

I grinned. "I've always wanted to revisit Africa. Did you figure out how to turn salt water into fresh water yet?" I said sarcastically. "And I love fresh sushi. You're such a great fisherman; I know you can provide for us."

He snorted while casting around a worried look.

"Seriously, rest your eyes and we'll take turns looking for the shark. I'll take the first shift."

I continued searching the vast ocean for any signs of life, staying alert for sharks and possible vessels in the distance. I let my feet dangle but I still had a firm grip on the raft. I tried to stay positive, but unwanted images of dying in the ocean entered my mind. Thoughts of sharks, dehydration, starvation, drowning, hurricane winds and losing my partner forced their way in as I determinedly pushed them back. *I'm a survivor,* I reminded myself. *But I'd like to use the wish I saved from last night. I want us to get rescued in one piece, preferably before morning.* I pictured Lucas and I back home having a beer at the end of the day, concentrating on good meditations. I envisioned us having a long life together, looking back at this moment as an interesting character-building experience.

I wondered about the statue. Did its crystal have supernatural power? An ability to harness energy across space and time? None of us could explain our sighting of the *SS Cotopaxi*. Maybe Henry was right about Atlantis. If the idol did have bad juju, it's back in the Atlantic where it belongs. "You can have it Poseidon," I whispered, just in case.

The sun dipped lower in the sky and I figured we had a few hours of sunlight remaining. A marlin jumped in the distance and I admired its beauty. My eyes felt heavy, but I refused to close them. Lucas had to rest with his injury, not me. If I only had an energy drink.

A slight buzz hummed through the quietness, an unnatural sound of a distant engine. The sound moved closer so I called out, "Honey, are you awake? Lucas, I hear an engine."

He lifted his head, slowly scanning the horizon. I followed his gaze.

"It's a helicopter! I can tell by the sound." We both stared at the sky, straining to see the source of the noise. As the buzz became louder and I recognized the distinct hum of the blades spinning. A black dot on the horizon quickly came into view. I sat upright and began waving. Lucas did the same. "It's a J-Hawk," he called out with enthusiasm. "That's what the Coast Guard uses."

I longed for a flare. I fumbled around in the side pocket of my khaki's for a small mirror I usually carry. I pulled it out, directing it towards the sun in hopes of creating a reflection. Lucas continued to wave his arms as I flashed the mirror.

The crew of the J-Hawk were in sight, with one wearing a mask and snorkel. They lowered a basket to our raft. Lucas grabbed it and lifted a VHF radio while continuing to hold on waiting for instructions.

"Captain, this is Coast Guard. We are unable to follow normal procedure and send a man in to help you. We are watching a large whitetip circling your life raft. It's too dangerous for our rescue swimmer to jump into the water. I'm going to need you to follow my instructions very carefully."

"I'm ready," Lucas shot back.

"We can only take one at a time." The voice said from the VHF. "It's best if you help the female into the basket, then we will send it back down for you."

"Come here baby." Lucas called out. "Crawl along the outside of the raft." I inched along the border like a prowling cat. He grabbed me, propelling me into the basket in one swoop.

"You should go first." I said. "You're injured."

"I'll be right up."

I sat in the container looking down into the bottomless ocean. Chopper blades were spraying Lucas with a shark aggressively closing in on him. "Hold on sweetie," I shouted. "He might bump again."

Within minutes I safely climbed aboard the helicopter and the basket lowered back down to pick up Lucas. I suddenly realized I was topless. One of the men put a blanket around me. I squeaked out a "Thank you."

"He's injured and might need a hospital." I held my breath. Glancing down I watched Lucas climb into the basket and ascend. The shark still circled.

Two Coast Guards helped him into the aircraft, removing my shirt from his head and examining his injuries. "Let's go to Jackson Memorial," I heard one of them say.

"How did you find us?" Lucas asked.

"We were on a routine patrol mission looking for human traffickers and drug runners when we got a call to be aware of a small plane ditching off Bimini."

"So I guess they heard my broadcast," Lucas said with satisfaction.

"We came to this spot to check out a strange luminous glow. There were green and pink colors all around the raft. I've never seen anything like it. It dissipated the moment we started lowering the rescue receptacle."

Uga-Bugga I inaudibly mouthed.

EPILOGUE

OCTOBER 10, 2011

COLUMBUS DAY REGATTA

"**D**amn Jamie, you're right this is crazy." I said, standing on the bow of the Kramers' Bertram.

Various music blared from hundreds of boats, including country from the Contender we rafted upon. A sea full of people, clothed and bare naked floated in between small and large vessels.

"Did you ever find out more information on the idol?" Jamie asked.

"I couldn't radiocarbon date it or source it. But I tracked down an important document while we were in Cuba. In the archives, I found a diary from a Santeria priestess. Her drawing was identical to our idol. She was adamant about its supernatural powers and truly believed it brought down the 1715 fleet. She also noted the green glow. She'd found it on the beach in Cuba, already carved."

"It doesn't sound like a coincidence to me."

"No, it doesn't. But the bigger question is where did it originate?"

"Russ, come on over." Lucas called out. "I need everyone in the saloon, I have rum runner's waiting."

A dozen beads of various colors and sizes swung around his neck as he climbed aboard the Bertram.

Lucas handed everyone a drink, "To friendship."

"Here, here." Nick said, taking a sip.

Lucas raised his glass towards me. "And to love." I smiled and realized he was now on one knee, holding a ring. "Raves will you marry me?"

I beamed. "Yes." I kissed the pink scar on his forehead and then his lips as he slipped the ring on my finger.

"Congratulations," The three cheered.

"Now, let's jump into the party." I said, and ran and dove off the stern.

THE END

ABOUT THE AUTHOR

Born and raised in Cincinnati and Northern Kentucky, I moved to Los Angeles as a young adult to follow my passion for culture, travel and education. I quickly discovered Archaeology and received my Master's Degree and a successful career in Southern California. I've always enjoyed writing and telling stories so several years ago I shifted my focus to writing. *Breakfast in Bimini* is my second novel.

I travel widely, but now call Florida home. Most of my writing takes place at our second home in Bimini, a small island in the Bahamas. I reside with my husband, and a diva dog named Yoda. I find sanity and peace in writing, running, yoga and piloting a small plane. I'm still passionate about Archaeology as evident in my novels.

Made in the USA
Monee, IL
20 April 2021